DEATH SENTENCES

MICHAEL ZIMECKI

CRIME WAVE PRESS

Crime Wave Press
Flat D, 11th Fl. Liberty Mansion
26E Jordan Road
Yau Ma Tei, Hong Kong
http://www.crimewavepress.com

ISBN 978 988 16557 8 3

Cover Design by Hans Kemp
Cover Illustration by Gerhard Joren

What will you do when they come to take your guns?

Andrew MacDonald (aka William Luther Pierce)

I'm gonna let the **AKA** can speak for me make your peace now.

French Montana

At first I started back, unable to believe that it was indeed I who was reflected in the mirror; and when I became fully convinced that I was in reality the monster that I am, I was filled with the bitterest sensations of despondence and mortification.

Mary Shelley

<u>Pop</u>

Y ou may remember him from the photograph in your daily paper, the one that rose, like dawn, above the fold, and was waiting there to greet you after the paper had landed, explosively, on your doorstep. In the photograph, one of his eyes cocked upward, peering at the headline in 66 pt. type at the top of the page, while the other (the lazy one) turned in toward the policeman beside him, the one escorting him from the courtroom past the reporters jammed into the hallway and into the pen, a brief stopover on his journey to the State Correctional Institute in Garrow County. The police officer sharing space with him in the photo permitted himself the barest of smiles, but the prisoner was expressionless (save for that cocked eye), revealing not the slightest hint of emotion (other than curiosity perhaps), and certainly no remorse or regret (even though, as anyone in the crowd assembled in the corridor would be sure to tell you, he had a lot to feel sorry for.) The judgment of the crowd, not to mention the jury that had convicted him, could be summed up by the terse, single-word headline that hung over his head (the one that screamed "DEATH!), which, come to think of it, also ingeminated the offenses that had caused him to be put on trial in the first place.

I am writing this book in honor of his crimes.

***

The day after Obama was elected president, Pop went out and bought himself an AK-47. (He called it his "choppa." He called the president "B.O.") Imported by Century Arms, the AK was Romanian-made and cost $422.25, after tax, but Pop figured it was a bargain. It would be worth a lot more than that after Obama restored the "assault weapons" ban, just like Beck and Hannity said he would after he took office.

His name was Peter Popovich but everyone called him Pop. They called him Pop because it was short for his last name, of course, but also because he was a year older than his contemporaries, having been held back in school by his mum (about whom I will have more to say later) and forced to repeat the fifth grade.

That's when things started to go bad for him. He was in the fifth grade when he discovered he had a penis and started to play with it all the time, or at least that's what his mummy thought. He was in the fifth grade when he learned that he was different from the other kids.

He learned this when he was out searching for night crawlers on the bank of a creek near his house with his friend Kenny G one day. (Pop called him Kenny G, even though there wasn't any "G" in Kenny's name and he didn't look at all like the smooth-jazz artist of the same name, at least not then, back in fifth grade. Later, Pop started calling him "KG" for short, which was an abbreviation for "Knee" and "Grow," and was intended as a joke. Pop's big revelation happened when Kenny G went around a bush to take a pee, and came back to find Pop holding the head of a frog on a stick. Jesus, Petey, KG said. Jesus. Pop took the head off the stick and threw it in the creek, and he and KG never talked about it again, but, from that point on, they both knew Pop was strange.

***

A brief word about the pen I am using to write this book. It consists of basically just the ink portion of a pen and a writing tip. This is what the screws – I'm sorry, they prefer to be referred to as correctional officers, or COs – provide to the inmates at SCI-Garrow, the ones on death row, that is, and the rationale behind it is to prevent the inmate from being able to use the pen as a weapon. (Without its housing, the pen can't be used to stab someone, unless, I guess, you could stick the tip into someone's eye (and good luck with that because it would be kind of like stabbing someone with a slinky.) They worry a lot about someone on death row getting a weapon. The concern, I guess, is that if someone on death row got a weapon, he wouldn't hesitate to use it. It's not like they could throw the book at him or anything by adding more years onto his sentence, if you know what I mean.

***

Another word or two about Pop when he was in the fifth grade. First, no one called him Pop back them. His mum, for example, always addressed him as Peter (never as "my son"), and the neighborhood kids took their cue from this, some of them, like his friend KG, calling him Petey, and others just calling him Pete. There was one kid who called him Peter Pan, which earned the kid a shiner, and another who called him Peterpeterpumpkineater, which didn't bother Pop as much. There was also a couple of kids who called him Pee-turd, and one, in particular, who called him Dickface, Cockmunch and Schlong, but these kids were bigger than Pop and he let them get away with it. For a brief time, right after he started the fifth grade again, some of the kids called him Repeat, and for an even briefer time he was even called Pistol Pete, after the basketball star, Pete Maravich (who, like him, was Serbian), but that didn't last long, and before too long everyone, even the bigger kids, called him Pop.

Second, Pop got his IQ tested when he was in the fifth grade, and found out it was 137. This astounded some of his teachers because Pop was getting Ds and Fs in most of his subjects, and it aroused the ire of his mum, who thought the test results merely confirmed her suspicion that he was jerking off. His mum's response to the IQ test was to ask the school to hold him back for another year, even though he could have probably gone on to the sixth grade, his grade point average being what it was, which wasn't great, but wasn't failing (at least not completely). Pop ended up spending the rest of his grade school years with younger kids who didn't like or trust him. Most of them were too afraid of him to actively shun him; they just stayed out of his way. This was especially true of the girls, who were jailbait anyway, those of them who were beginning to grow breasts and menstruate. Most of the time, he ate his lunch alone, and there wasn't anyone to exchange notes with, and even his locker partner tended to avoid him. It went on like that until he was in the eleventh grade, when he got tired of being a social outcast. He dropped out and found himself a job working for a Jewish shopkeeper on the

Hill, which was when he first found out about the New World Order and the plan to put people in concentration camps like Guantanamo, only right here in the United States.

But, whoa, I am getting way ahead of myself. There was another one, two, three, four … six years between fifth grade and his discovery and another eight until he acted on the knowledge. Plus he didn't gain his political insight all at once: first he discovered how greedy Jews were, then he learned about the international Jewish conspiracy and the grip it had on the financial markets, and then he learned about the plans to put people, dissidents like himself, in camps. Shit, Guantanamo wasn't opened until 2002, long after he had repeated the fifth grade, and it was only a year or so before he committed the crimes that landed him on death row, when he had learned that FEMA was constructing detention camps in Wyoming and Michigan and even in Pennsylvania, where he lived. In between, between the emotion and the response, as it were, there was a lot of stuff that happened, like his grandfather's death, and that thing between him and his landlord over the landlord's dog, and of course the whole sordid business with Keilah, who was his girlfriend and whom he probably should have shot.

***

All of the people on death row in Pennsylvania have killed someone, some by stabbing, some by stomping or strangling their victims, but most, the vast majority, with a gun. One of the men here used two steak knives to hack a woman to death inside her SUV and another guy used his hands to strangle a three-year-old before putting the child's body in a plastic garbage bag and throwing it into a creek. But, as I said, the weapon of choice was a gun. Most just picked up a gun and went on a rampage.

There are approximately 225 people on death row in Pennsylvania. The number goes up as more people are sent here and goes down as people die. Most of the people on death row die of natural causes while they are awaiting execution. In fact, the state has only executed three people since 1978. All three terminated their appeals, and asked the state to end their lives.

I may do the same when I am finished with this book. Life on death row isn't quite the picnic that people (you people) on the outside think it is. I get two books a week to read and have a TV, but that's all I have, besides my standard issue prison jumpsuit, my shoes, two pair of underwear and some other shit that I keep in a record-sized box, about the size of a small orange crate, next to my bed. I keep this manuscript in the box when I'm not working on it, along with the books, my flexi pen and some legal papers from my lawyer (wedged in next to the TP, a bar of soap, my shower sandals, and of course my glasses, the large prescription ones with the Fresnel lenses that I keep in the box when I'm not wearing them.) That's it. I can't put any munchies or other crap in the box because food isn't allowed in the cells, except at meal time, when it is delivered to me through the pie hole in the stainless steel door that separates my cell from the rest of G block and isolates me from the rest of the known world.

My cell measures 6' x 9' (believe me, I know. I've paced it over and over again) and I am not allowed out of it, except to see an occasional visitor, use the prison library, take a shower and exercise. I don't get many visitors. My Mum Evelyn couldn't be bothered to drive the one-and-a-half hours from Pittsburgh to Mononga, where the prison is located, and I have never had a single visit – not one – from her at all. My best friend KG came to see me a couple of times, then he got busted for driving under the influence and recklessly endangering another person. Luckily for Kenny, he got probation, but prison rules prohibit contact with anyone who is currently under parole or probation supervision. Maybe when he finishes probation, KG can pay me another visit, if he has a mind to.

It goes without saying that I am handcuffed and manacled when I am taken outside my cell for the two hours a day that I am permitted to leave. I exercise alone, of course, and I never speak to anyone, not even the COs. When I first got here, they cursed at me and called me names, but now they barely give me the time of day. It reminds me an awful lot of fifth grade.

***

His grandfather didn't like blacks or Jews or Asians or Hispanics or queers, but he liked Pop. Of course, he didn't tell Pop that he liked him, except for that one time a few days before he died, when he leaned his shoulder into Pop's and whispered in Pop's ear that he had been more like a son to him than his own son, Evelyn's brother, Stanislaw (Everyone called him, "Stan.") That almost went without saying, because Stan was a complete degenerate, a shiftless falling-down drunk who didn't care about anyone other than himself. When he was still alive, Stan wouldn't give Pop-Pop the time of day, which was just fine with Grandpop, who wouldn't trust Stan with his watch or any of his other temporal possessions.

Grand-pop's name was Victor, but no one called him that. His cronies called him Vic or Vickie, which made grand pop get all red. Grand-pop's brother, Uncle Paulie, called him Tory, which Grand-pop didn't like any better than Vickie. For reasons she never explained and that were completely opaque to Pop, Granny Popovich called him Sugar. (After her stroke, she called everyone Sugar, Pop later recalled.) For his part, Pop called his Grand-pop Pop-Pop, or Pop, for short, which confused the hell out of everyone after Pop failed the fifth grade and got his own nickname. Grand-pop and Pop kind of went with this, both responding to the same name for a while. Then Pop's mum, Evelyn, adopted the appellation Gran had used for Grand-pop, calling him Sugar, and then, finally, Sugar-Pop, which was the name that stuck in the Popovich household.

There was quite some irony in this because Grandpa Popovich was anything but sweet. It was that motherfucking nigger and that tight-assed Jew and that cocksucking faggot all day long with him. His total vocabulary must have contained about one hundred words and at least seventy-five of them were dirty.

Pop-Pop (this was before he became Sugar-Pop) taught his grandson that blacks were shiftless and lazy and Jews were greedy. Although there weren't any Asians or Hispanics in their neighborhood, not at that time, Pop-Pop had served in the Army during World War II, and had fought the Japs in the Pacific. After the war, he served for a time with the military police in Tokyo. This experience lent him sufficient authority to opine that the Japs, although industrious, unlike the blacks, were not to be trusted. They were slant-eyed yellow bastards who worshipped false gods and would just as soon as stab you in the back as pretend they were your friends. Pop-Pop lamented the aid the U.S. poured into Japan after the war, and he credited himself with having the foresight to predict that the Japs would copy American products and mimic American technology and beat the U.S. at its own game.

Although he hated Japs as intensely as he hated blacks and Jews, Pop-Pop experienced some mild cognitive dissonance on this front, as he had found himself feeling compassion for the vanquished Japanese he met during his tenure with the MPs. He recalled fondly the family that invited him into their home and presented him with a book made of rice paper that was filled with pictographs and other indecipherable imagery. Pop-Pop had kept the book and occasionally brought it out for his grandson to see, holding the rice-paper manuscript in his rough hands as if it were a kite, or butterfly's wings, or some other fragile and delicate thing.

Pop-Pop also recalled with unsentimental detachment how he had attempted to tap his cigarette ash into the urn containing one of the Japanese family's ancestors and the horrified looks on the faces of his hosts as he reached out to do so. Fortunately, their looks froze him and the ash fell, unceremoniously, on a rice mat covering the portion of the living room floor under the mantle where the urn and its sacred contents rested.

After the war ended, Pop-Pop was known, for a brief period of time, as Victorious. His family and friends welcomed the returning hero, and, for a while, there was no place he could go without being greeted by thundering claps on the back from the men and petite kisses and discreet hugs (that was as good as it got) from the women. The best part of being a returning hero was the free shots and beers he received at his local watering hole. Soon, however, the tap shut off, and the back slaps, hugs and kisses stopped. Like his father before him, Pop-Pop took a job at the local steel mill, something he had sworn he would not do, and something he hated. One day, in a pique he took a swing at his foreman with a roundhouse right and was promptly fired, even though his punch had failed to connect with the foreman's face. The next day, Pop-Pop re-enlisted and got sent to Japan.

The Japan saga we have already visited. Pop learned little more concerning his grand-pop's service in Tokyo beyond the stories we have already shared with you about the Japanese family and the rice paper book and the urn. There was one other story (actually, two), narratives that Pop-Pop kept to himself and that only came tumbling out of him after a long night of binge drinking.

The first involved something he witnessed.

The second involved something somebody else saw.

Pop-Pop blurted out the first after he vomited on the floor, and slipped in his own vomit, and rolled around in it for a while. Help! He screamed. When no one answered, he called out for his wife, and then, a little bit later, for his daughter. No one came running. Gran was pissed because Pop-Pop hadn't told her he would be not only late but toasted, and she hated it when he went out drinking anyway. Evelyn didn't help because, well, because she was Evelyn and couldn't be bothered. Pop peeked at his grand pop from behind a door. Jesus Christ, Pop-Pop said. I feel like I'm back in Japan again. His grandson hadn't a clue what he meant by this, but his curiosity had been stoked sufficiently to come out from his hiding place and hand Pop-Pop a towel. Later, after his grandson had wiped the vomit off his face and given him an aspirin, Pop-Pop told him about the time when he was stationed at GHQ in Tokyo and watched two other MPs pat down a Jap who worked as a translator at the Dai-Ichi-Seimei Building (Pop-Pop called it the Die Icky Semen Building), where MacArthur had his headquarters. The Jap must have said something the MPs didn't like because they started to slap the Jap around a bit, and he said something back, and the next thing Pop-Pop knew they were holding the man by the ankles and dumping his head into the moat around the Imperial Palace, the main residence of the Emperor of Japan, which was situated close to the Dai-Ichi Seimei Building. Pop-Pop thought they were going to drown the man. Each time his head came out of the water, he let out a little whimper, and the MPs would dunk him back down again. On one of the man's trips out of the water, he saw Pop-Pop (upside down, of course) and cried out something in English. Then the man's head went down again, and he came up gasping for air. The third time his head came out of the water, Pop-Pop figured out that the man was asking him for help. Pop-Pop wanted to help, he really did, but he didn't want to cross his fellow MPs, who were just doing their job so to speak. So Pop-Pop just stood and watched while the MPs continued to abuse the man. Eventually, the man stopped saying anything, and his face went all blue, and the MPs dumped him into the moat and didn't lift him back out again. After the MPs let go of the man's feet, Pop-Pop searched the surface of the water. He thought he saw the man's yellow head bobbing in the water, but he wasn't sure, and he didn't want to risk diving into the moat and drowning himself, not for some damned Jap.

As to the second story, it was related to Pop-Pop by a Polish priest. The priest was in charge of an orphanage on the outskirts of Hiroshima, where the first atom bomb was dropped. Afterward, the priest went to Hiroshima to see if he could help and witnessed first-hand the damage caused by the bomb. The Polish priest related a scene of almost unimaginable horror. The blast had disintegrated virtually every structure within a radius of over a mile, and the ensuing fireball spread destruction outward from the hypocenter. The city's asphalt infrastructure curdled like chips on a griddle. Hiroshima was in flames.

After the fires ebbed, the priest walked the smoldering terrain. Hiroshima was like a burned forest after the trees were gone, all black and stumpy, and, for a moment, he wondered where the people went. The Polish priest saw the shadow of a man etched on concrete in the spot where the man had been standing right before he got vaporized. Then he noticed a hand sticking out from the ground. It wasn't waving or anything, but the priest grabbed it anyway (why, Pop didn't know, because it sounded like an icky thing to do) and found that it was attached to a body. He spent the rest of the day pulling bodies out from under the ashes that carpeted the ground, stacking the dead in piles. Many of the dead had their clothes blown off, revealing the ruddy brown nuclear tan caused by radiation exposure or the striated patches of skin where the heat from the thermal pulse had been reflected and absorbed by the colors of the garments they had had been wearing.

Pop Pop cursed the Japanese for inviting this destruction upon themselves. If it weren't for the atom bomb, he reckoned, hundreds of thousands of G.I.s would have died in an invasion of Japan. The death of even one American soldier was too great a sacrifice to pay even if it meant the deaths of thousands of Japanese civilians. For the rest of his life, Pop-Pop never questioned the decision to use the bomb, and he held those who did in the utmost contempt. There were times, however, when his sleep was disturbed by memories of what the Polish priest had told him and he would awake stammering to his grandson, "Why is the heart of man so dark?"

Pop didn't have any answers for him then, and he doesn't now.

***

According to a pamphlet I found on a table in the prison library, the State Correctional Institute at Garrow was built in the early 1990s, but was modeled on a penal system that was more than two centuries old. Called the Pennsylvania system, it was promoted by the Quakers and based on the principle that solitary confinement fosters penitence and encourages reformation. It was eventually superseded and replaced by the Auburn system, whatever that is, because in the opinion of many penologists, the Pennsylvania system had a deleterious effect on the minds of prisoners.

Solitary confinement, and here I am quoting from an inmate's brief, has been known to worsen an inmate's pre-existing mental problems or to cause mental illness where none had been observed before. Some psychiatrists even maintain that prolonged solitary confinement can induce a syndrome, similar to an organic brain syndrome, called segregation psychosis and characterized by hyper-responsivity to external stimuli; perceptual distortions, illusions and hallucinations, panic attacks; difficulty with thinking, concentration and memory; intrusive obsessional thoughts; problems with impulse control; the emergence of primitive aggressive ruminations; and overt paranoia. There is a growing body of empirical evidence that solitary confinement causes permanent or semi-permanent changes to brain physiology. EEG studies have shown diffuse slowing of brain waves in prisoners after just a week of solitary confinement.

Some legal scholars believe that solitary confinement is a psychological form of torture. Most people, of course, don't get too bent out of shape over what goes on in prisons. Most people figure that inmates, especially those on death row, have it coming to them, and boo-hoo, if their life isn't all peachy keen.

Solitary confinement, as practiced at SCI-Garrow, does not mean that the inmate is alone. He is alone in his cell for 22 to 23 hours at a stretch, but he is not truly alone because he is under constant video surveillance. To make it easier for the camera to see him, the light in his cell is on virtually at all times, and it is a violation of prison rules, one that will risk having your few small privileges stripped away, to do anything to try to dim it. Sometimes, the COs will cut you a little bit of a break and dim the light at night, but it is on all the time, and the only thing that varies is its intensity.

When I first got here, I was afraid to touch myself for fear that someone might be watching. Then I had my first wet dream since I was fourteen. If that doesn't beat all hell, I thought. Now I hack my pud whenever I want and I don't care who's looking. Shit, if masturbation was a crime, I'd be on death row.

***

For Pop's mum, of course, masturbation was a crime. Pop probably would have done a whole lot better in school if his mum had left him alone instead of barging into his room all the time to try to catch him jacking off. Yeah, mum, he'd say, as he looked up from his geometry text, I'm reading a db. After a while, Pop figured he might as well be reading a dirty book, or looking at a Playboy centerfold than waiting for his mum to interrupt him in the middle of a word problem.

Not that he was all that focused on his school work. Pop had this problem, called amblyopia, more commonly known as lazy eye. His left eye was the lazy one. It would drift off in space or just go a little vacant while his right eye trained on the task at hand, looking where it was supposed to look, and Pop guessed it made him seem a little goofy, which probably explained why he hadn't had any success with girls up to this point in his life. (For a while, when he was very young, he wore a patch over his good eye, which must have been a real hit with all the chicks in pre-school, but his mum told him he was constantly taking it off and it got to be so much of a pain for her, she decided not to bother.

Later, a school nurse referred him to an optometrist, who prescribed some glasses that had a prism in them. They were large and black, which didn't help him with the girls, and every time Pop wore them he saw rainbows. This wasn't good for a kid of eastern European descent because rainbows symbolize renewed hope and thus cut against the genetic grain of fatalism. In an amazing display of optimism and trust, Pop hung onto the prescription and kept getting it refilled as he got older, even though he hardly ever wore the prism glasses anymore.)

The amblyopia probably helped to explain why Pop wasn't much of a scholar. To be sure, it didn't really affect his vision (because his right eye compensated for his left one.) He could see just fine (especially when he was staring at a classmate's tits.) However, Pop sometimes had problems with depth perception and occasionally got double vision, especially when he was feeling tired (hence the prism glasses). He didn't use his lazy eye as an excuse for his poor school performance, but Pop earnestly believed (although he had no ophthalmologic evidence to support his belief) that reading strained his eye, the poor one, making it harder for him to do his homework. In any event, Pop didn't like doing homework and sometimes found it was easier to give up on school assignments than to persevere and finish them.

By the time Pop got to high school he'd had enough of the bullshit that passes for education anyway. Then his grand pop got sick, and he thought, maybe, he should stick around to help out. His Gran was too feeble and strokey to be of any use (hell, she needed help herself), and his mum was always drunk. So Pop just up and announced one day that he was quitting school. No, you're not, mum said. Yes, I am, he told her, and he subverted her authority by refusing to go. Finally, after Pop missed or was late for school so many times that the authorities threatened to charge his mum for violating the law on compulsory attendance, Evelyn relented and signed the papers that allowed him to drop out.

Pop was cheered by the (seeming) totality of Evelyn's capitulation and he felt smug over his victory in the global war between mum and son. Plus, he really truly loved his grand pop and really truly wanted to help. He soon realized, however, that he had made a major miscalculation. Not going to school meant that he had to spend even more time at home with mum. Pop and Evelyn argued on a daily basis. Her son was always sleeping in too late. He didn't help out with the house work. He didn't do his chores, why, he wasn't even doing enough to help Sugar-Pop. (Smoking Sugar's cigarettes, Mum admonished him, wasn't help.) These offenses were venial sins, but another was mortal: Pop wasn't making a significant contribution to the household. By this, his mum meant that he wasn't earning any money.

Evelyn soon found a way to rectify the situation. Look at this, she said, one morning after Pop had slept in late, as she pulled the covers from his bed and opened the shades to let the sun shine in. Pop squinted, his eyes tearing up from the light filling the room. Here, look at this, she said. Pop was still struggling to focus his vision – he was about to quip it must be true that masturbation can make one go blind – when his mum thrust the morning newspaper in front of his face. The paper was folded to a page in the classified section where Evelyn had drawn a large red circle with a flow pen around an advertisement for a job. Pop's swimming eyes couldn't make out what the newsprint said, so his mum grabbed the paper from him and read the ad aloud. It said, "STOCK BOY. NO EXPERIENCE NECESSARY." Pop's mum insisted he apply for the job. Pop scratched at the stubble on his face. Or else? He spat. Or else I'll kick your lazy ass out of my house.

In point of fact, the house wasn't Evelyn's – it belonged to Pop-Pop and Gran. But mum wasn't a stickler for details. And the problem was she meant what she said. Pop knew that she meant it because she almost immediately went to the phone and started to call the cops. What are you doin' mum? he asked. Calling 911 to tell the cops to haul your lazy fucking ass out of here. Now wait a sec, Pop said, as he sat up in bed and let his feet touch the floor. What do you want to do that for? Pressing "9" on the telephone keypad, Evelyn chose to let her fingers do the talking. (The fashion nail on her finger, the one she used to hit the keypad, was colored red, Pop noticed.) Think about it, mum, he pleaded. I mean, where would I go? I don't know, Evelyn said. Maybe you can move in with your friend, Kenny, and his parents, or maybe you can go out and find your good-for-nothing dad and live with him.

Evelyn touched the "1" key on the telephone.

Pop thought for a moment about reaching out and grabbing the phone from her hand, but he wasn't sure he could get there in time, and he didn't know what would happen if the call got through and the 911 operator heard a struggle. Can they trace the call that fast? he wondered. And what would he do if the cops actually came?

Evelyn's finger hovered over the keypad.

Okay, alright, already. I'll apply for the job.

Fifteen minutes later, Pop was dressed and on a bus to Uptown. He got out on Forbes Avenue and walked around for a bit until he located the address in the ad. The sign over the storefront said, "Ralph's Discount City – Men's Clothing." Pop stood in front of the store, working up his courage, and then he went in and asked for Ralph.

"There ain't no Ralph here," a clerk at the front of the store said.

Flustered and perplexed, Pop stuck his hands in his pockets and turned around and left the store. Back on the sidewalk, he pulled the ad from his jacket where he had stuffed it, and checked the store address again. It matched. Pop stared at the ad for a couple of minutes before going back inside the store.

The clerk he had spoken to was waiting on a customer. Pop used the time to look around. He saw a rack of shirts that were popular in the 1970s. There were suits on display made of polyester. There was some other stuff – clip suspenders and wide ties with big polka dots – but there wasn't anything that anyone in his right mind would wear. Everything was on sale, however, and everything was cheap. A sign in a corner said: MARKED DOWN – 50% TO 70% OFF.

"There still ain't nobody here named Ralph," the sales clerk said as Pop stepped toward him. Pop thrust his hand into his jacket and pulled out the crumpled Help Wanted ad and handed it to the clerk.

Oh, you want to talk to Saul, he said. Then the clerk led Pop to a room in the back and introduced him to a short, balding fat man seated behind a desk. The man had a big black bushy mustache that looked like it hadn't been clipped in weeks. His name was Saul Savage and he was the owner of Ralph's. Pop extended a hand toward him, but Saul declined to shake it, motioning Pop to sit down in a chair next to the desk.

The interview lasted all of five minutes. Mr. Savage

asked if Pop had ever done stock work before. Pop said no. The store owner asked if Pop had any kind of prior work experience. Pop told him he hadn't. Mr. Savage asked him what he was good at, and Pop, shrugging his shoulders, said he didn't know. How old are you, kid? Mr. Savage asked with an incredulous smile, front teeth showing through his soup strainer. Pop said he was 17, soon to be 18, and that he had dropped out of school. Mr. Savage looked at Pop as if he were inspecting a bug through a microscope. Then he asked Pop if he thought he could get a letter from the school district verifying that he was 17 and had withdrawn from school. I guess so, Pop said. Minimum wage to start, no fringe benefits, Mr. Savage said. I'll give you 20 hours a week at first, and if you're punctual, come to work on time, don't call off when you are scheduled, maybe more hours later, maybe we'll see if you're any good at sales. Get the letter, bring it in, and I'll put you to work in the stockroom right away.

THE POLITICIZATION OF PETER POPOVICH, PART 1

When he was lying on the ground with a bullet in his leg and thinking about putting a bullet in his brain – this was after he had committed the crimes that caused him to be put in SCI-Garrow – Pop bargained with himself about whether he should live or die. If he died, the whole fucking business would be over, but if he lived he might tell his story one day. Pop told himself that if he lived, he would write a novel. It would tell the world how he became who he was and why he did the things he did – under a fictional veneer, of course. Pop also told himself he would write about things that nobody else writes about. Like work.

Americans work longer and harder than any other people on the face on the planet. According to The Reader's Digest, or some such other rag, the average American spends 8.4 hours a day working (more than the Germans or the Japanese, or the lazy, cigarette-smoking, sex-obsessed French – more than anybody else, in fact), and this statistic doesn't even count the time that Americans spend commuting to work, or just thinking about it, or waking up from nightmares about it as they toss and turn in their sleep.

You might think American literature would have a lot to say about American workers and their jobs. You'd be wrong. Hemingway wrote about bullfighting, and Mailer wrote about war, and Phillip Roth wrote about masturbating with a piece of liver, but none of them had squat to say about work. (John Dos Passos wrote about work, but no one reads him anymore. Pop did. Pop read the first volume of Dos Passos' great trilogy, U.S.A., because he was attracted to its title. He particularly loved the part about Fainy and Doc Bingham, which was social truth about what it is like to be used in the workplace by some greedy, lying son-of-a-bitch.)

Which brings us to Mr. Savage. Mr. Savage was a genius at getting other people to do the work and making himself rich. Take Ralph. Ralph was the guy who started Ralph's Discount City – Men's Clothes. Using money he had inherited from his dad, Mr. Savage partnered with Ralph and took over the business after

Ralph's psychiatrist told him he would never get over the panic attacks he had on almost a daily basis until he severed his relationship with Mr. Savage. You gotta divorce this guy, you just gotta, Ralph's shrink said. If you don't, you're gonna die. So Ralph offered to sell the business to Mr. Savage, and Mr. Savage agreed to buy it – at a huge discount. And that's why there wasn't any Ralph when Pop Popovich came to Ralph's Discount City – Men's Clothing to inquire about a job there. (It's also why "Ralph" and "Discount" were still part of the store's name, Pop figured.)

That, at any rate, was the story related to Pop by Marge, who claimed to have heard it from Mr. Savage himself. Marge was Mr. Savage's Girl Friday (although at age 42, she was hardly a girl) and she basically ran Ralph's. Marge did the books. She trained the sales clerks (there was a lot of turnover). Marge placed the advertising specials in the daily newspaper and had circulars printed to hand out in the streets. About the only thing Marge didn't do was buy the stuff they sold; Mr. Savage, with his hideous taste in clothes, did that, but Marge managed the inventory, reordering when stocks were low, tagging and pricing the merchandise and arranging the displays. She also was constantly arguing with Mr. Savage about ordering merchandise they couldn't move (those clip-on suspenders, for instance), invariably losing those arguments.

Marge was the one who took Pop by the hand his first day on the job and showed him what to do. The merchandise they sold came off trucks in boxes or on wholesale clothing racks. Pop would haul the boxes and the racks into the basement, where the inventory was kept, and after Marge had tagged and priced it, Pop would take it upstairs and put it in the retail fittings – on the display shelves and so forth. Most of his time, the vast majority of it, was spent in the basement cutting up boxes with a Stanley knife or folding up plastic and hauling it out to the trash.

The job was pretty tedious, and occasionally involved some pretty heavy lifting, but Pop didn't mind it, and he especially like being in the basement by himself. It gave him space to think.

One of the things he thought about was the division of labor he observed in the store. He thought it was unfair that Marge did practically everything and got paid less than everybody else (except Pop). He thought it was unfair that Mr. Savage did virtually nothing and made more money than anybody else (particularly Pop).

Pop's basement ruminations became angry, roiling thoughts after Pop got his first paycheck and found that it was short. He went to talk to Mr. Savage about it, and Mr. Savage told him he had been docked for being late. Twice. Pop promised to be more punctual. He showed up on time every workday for two weeks in a row, and didn't leave until he was told it was all right to go. Despite all this, his paycheck was short again. Flustered, he went to Mr. Savage to complain for a second time.

Mr. Savage looked up from the pulp magazine he was reading at his desk. On Thursday, he said, our shipment was late, and, as a result, there was nothing for you to do. I can't pay you for standing around doing nothing. But I was here! Pop protested. It's not my fault the shipment was late. Plus, you would have docked me if I hadn't been here. Look, it's simple, Mr. Savage said in a patronizing tone of voice. No work, no pay.

After this meeting, in which he got no satisfaction whatsoever, Pop groused to one of the sales clerks about what Mr. Savage had done. Just be thankful you're not working on commission, the clerk said. You'd more than likely starve.

Pop didn't think there was much to be thankful for because Mr. Savage always found a way to make his paycheck lighter than it should have been. He thought about quitting, but he knew it wouldn't go over well with his mum. One night after dinner, when mum was out, Pop told his grand pop about his problems at work. "What did you expect?" his grand pop said, as he sucked oxygen through the cannula hooked up to his nose. "He's a Jew, ain't he?" grand pop snorted.

Pop happened to repeat his grand pop's opinion to Marge one day at work. Why, Peter, she said, addressing him formally. I'm surprised at you.

Pop was surprised, too, at her reaction, particularly in light of the treatment Marge received from Mr. Savage, and he wanted to draw her out on the issue. But he hadn't read The Turner Diaries or The International Jew or None Dare Call It Conspiracy or Behold a Pale Horse or any of the other books that would help to form his later views, and his thinking on the subject was still in what you might call the embryonic stage. Plus, he didn't want to offend Marge because she had been helpful to him in his early days on the job, and still functioned as something of a buffer between him and Mr. Savage.

What's more, Pop had the hots for her daughter.

She was a year older than Pop and was a student at CCAC, the local community college, where she was studying to be a nurse. She had long brown hair and the greatest pair of legs Pop had ever seen. They first met on Serbian Day at Kennywood, an amusement park, while Pop was waiting to ride the Exterminator, a roller coaster in which the rider sits in a small car while it races around a steel track (The Kennywood ride invited the rider to imagine that he, or she, was a rat being chased around the track by group of exterminators.) It was a popular ride and the line was long. Pop felt himself getting warm and sticky in the afternoon sun. He was mopping the sweat from his forehead with the crown of his ball cap when he felt someone suddenly pinch his elbow. He turned around and saw Marge. Hi, Pop, she said. Then she introduced him to her daughter. It was a hello-how-are-you kind of meeting, too brief and cursory for any kind of electricity to pass between them. Pop did notice, as Keilah walked away, that she had a really nice body on her, and wished he had found something clever to say to her before she and her mom said goodbye.

A few days later, Marge asked Pop he was interested in a pair of tickets to a concert by some third or fourth rate band. Marge had been given the tickets by Mr. Savage, who got them from an ad rep. If Pop didn't have a friend to go with, maybe he could take Keilah to the concert? Pop didn't have the slightest interest in the band, but he did have an interest in Keilah. So he said yes, and they went out.

They hit it off. Keilah was attracted to the swagger of Pop's bad boy pose. And Pop was simply bowled over. Keilah was pretty and she was smart, but not pretentious or snotty, and Pop found she was easy to talk to. Hell, he didn't know before he met her that he could even so much as talk to a girl. Pretty soon, he was shucking and jiving with her all the time, and spending so much time at Marge's house, he practically lived there. Found yerself another place to stay, mum said with a smirk.

Marge seemed to welcome Pop's presence in her household. She didn't have a husband (Pop didn't know why) and she and Keilah lived alone. Pop felt like a welcome guest. He assumed Marge liked having a man around the house. He did small household chores, the heavy lifting kind, and was a frequent invitee to dinner. One afternoon, while Marge was at work and he was off, Pop snuggled up to Keilah on the couch in Marge and Keilah's living room. He got her bra off and had his tongue in her mouth when Marge came home early and found them engaged on the sofa. Get out, she said, pointing a finger at Pop, and sounding every bit like his mum. Later, he and Keilah had a blow-up on the phone.

To top things off, Pop had a run-in with Mr. Savage the next day on the job. One of the sales clerks picked up one of Mr. Savage's magazines and Pop's utility knife fell out, slicing the man's hand, which bled profusely. What the hell? Saul Savage said before he drove the clerk to Central Medical to have his hand checked out. Mr. Savage had been on Pop's case about closing the knife up when he was finished using it, fully retracting the blade within its die-cast metal handle and leaving it on a basement shelf. Mr. Savage didn't know why the blade hadn't been retracted or what it was doing between the pages of a magazine sitting on his office table. What's more, Pop couldn't give him a satisfactory explanation. You're fired, Mr. Savage said as Pop fumbled for the words to convey how truly sorry he felt.

Pop got fired on a Friday. His grand pop died two days later. Pop wasn't home when it happened. He had gone to Emlenton with Kenny G to spend the weekend at his friend's camp, and he and KG spent all day Saturday and Sunday drinking beer. After they had sucked all of the fluid out of the cans, Kenny and Pop set them up on a fence and shot holes in them with KG's .22. It felt small in his hand, and Pop wished he had a Chief's Special or a 9-milimeter to shoot with instead. Something with more pop than Kenny G's small caliber hand gun. Still, it was fun to shoot the cans, almost as much fun as drinking beer. It helped to vent some of Pop's frustration. He pretended he was shooting Mr. Savage instead of a can of Bud.

When he got home that Monday, Evelyn told him to put on a clean shirt and find a tie, and he drove with her to Cmjanski's, where Sugar-Pop was laid out. He actually looked better in his cheap suit with all the funeral makeup on his face than he had looked the last time Pop had seen him. (Pop almost didn't recognize him without the oxygen cannula in his nose.) In his last days, Sugar had been falling down a lot, and the last time Pop saw him he had cuts and bruises all over his arms and legs and a huge scratch on his right cheek. (It was practically invisible when Pop was viewing him in his casket.) The last time Pop was with him, Sugar had also soiled himself. Pop cleaned him up and got him into a fresh change of clothes (not as nice as the suit he was wearing in his casket, but better than the smelly pants he had been wearing before Pop helped him get changed.) That's when Sugar told him he was a good boy, that he had been more like a son to him than Stan had ever been. Pop nodded his head gratefully. Then he made his grandfather a sandwich and got him something to drink. Petey, Sugar said, as he sipped milk through a straw, I don't want to die alone. Pop told him not to worry, that he would be there for him, that he could always count on Pop. That's why he felt real bad when he found out that Sugar had died while he was away.

Never again, Pop told himself. From that point on in time, he'd never renege on a promise, no matter the consequences, no matter what it cost. Promises are meant to be kept – isn't that what Frost said in that stupid little poem of his about the woods filled up with snow? From that point on in time, Pop Popovich was true to his word. Honest he was. And if you don't believe that, just ask his mum, she'll tell you. She knows. Evelyn Popovich was there the day Pop kept the promise that landed him in this cell.

<u>Mummy</u>

Pop wasn't the first person in his family to kill someone. That distinction belonged to his mum. His mummy, Evelyn, didn't actually shoot or stab someone. That wouldn't have been her style. She killed someone the way most women do, by getting someone else to do it for her

The victim's name was Ray. He was Pop's cousin, once removed, and Evelyn got involved with him after Pop's father left. Although he didn't know for sure, Pop suspected they were sleeping around, which would be incest, technically speaking, and which really creeped him out. In Evelyn's defense, Ray was an alcoholic like herself and they were drinking buddies before they became fuck buddies, if indeed they ever were.

Their relationship was pretty tempestuous. They fought each other all they time, probably over who would get the last swig from the bottle they shared in the alley. (Gran wouldn't let mummy drink in the house, but she did anyway, out of spite.) Once, during an argument, Ray broke Evelyn's nose and she nearly poked out his eye and they both ended up in the County jail for public drunkenness. (Except for Pop's father, just about every man that Evelyn had ever been with had busted up a part of her, her nose, a rib or two, her jaw. Pieces of her were strewn across several counties.) After Evelyn came home she got a Protection from Abuse Order to keep Ray away. Three days later, she woke up in her bedroom and found him standing over her. All hell broke loose. Evelyn started screaming at Ray at the top of her lungs, and Ray started busting up the furniture. Fortunately, one of the neighbors called the police before the argument got really physical, and they cops grabbed Ray and put him in jail for violating the PFA. (They also took his guns, a topic we will revisit later.)

The night of the big brewhaha was the last time Pop saw Ray. He saw him as the cops were putting the cuffs on him and taking him away. As far as Pop was concerned, it was good riddance (although he did feel a tiny sliver of sympathy for poor Ray as he was led away by the Men in Blue, one officer practically dragging him into the paddy wagon while the other poked Ray in the back with his baton.) Whether Ray and Evelyn ever hooked up again, Pop couldn't say. But he could tell you that Ray went to live with one of the alkies he met in the halfway house after he got out of jail. Ray and his alky pal got themselves an apartment in Beechview. Ray was paying his half of the rent with the cash assistance he got from the county and he and his alkie buddy, whose name was Johnny, were getting along okay. Yep, things were going swimmingly in alkie paradise land until Ray got tanked on too much Thunderbird and decided that he needed to see Pop's mum. Johnny went ballistic. You can't do that, he said. The cops will pick you up for violating your PFA, and they'll put you in County, and you'll lose your welfare, and I'll lose this apartment and be out on the fuckin' street. Sorry, that's life, Ray said, but I've got to see Eve. He had one foot out of the apartment when Johnny cracked him with a bat in the back of the head, then dragged him back inside and began to beat the crap out of him. By the time Johnny was done, Ray was a bloody pulp. He was unconscious and hardly breathing, but he might have survived if Johnny had called the paramedics right away. Instead, he sat down and finished off the T-bird and smoked what was left in Ray's pack of cigarettes, and waited nearly two hours before he dialed 911. A year or so later, a jury blamed him for Ray's death.

Pop figured there was plenty of blame to go around, starting with Ray's father, Radovan, who married grand pop's sister, Zora, and walked out on her a few months after Ray was born. Zora died while Ray was in high school – from a broken heart, Sugar said – and Ray dropped out to join the Navy. It was all downhill from there. Ray must have got more of his genes from his father than from his mother, or at least the dominant ones, because he took after his father, Radovan, and resembled him even closer the older he became. Radovan, or Radek, as he was known, was a bum. A flat-out, simple-ass bum. You could see him every day on Carson Street, bummin' nickels and dimes and quarters from anyone who would give him some change (to get somethin' to eat, he'd say, but he really meant he needed another drink.) Sometimes, you could hear him sobbing in the alley where he slept, crying out to Zora, his poor departed wife, moaning piteously about how much he still loved and missed her (when in reality, he had helped to speed her to her grave.) It was no wonder, in short, that Ray became an alcoholic. First, he had all this grief hanging like a cloud over his head. Second, his father was an alcoholic, as was his grandfather before him and his great grand dad, too, some guy from Serbia (Pop thought his name was Darko) who got off the boat at Ellis Island holding a bottle of potato vodka in his hand.

If you were looking for someone to blame, of course, Evelyn also fit the bill. Luckily for her, her name was never mentioned in the newspaper story about the trial, although the paper did report that Johnny beat Ray to death because he was going to see a woman in the Heights who had a PFA against him. Pop suspected that the neighbors knew who the mystery woman really was. They didn't need to see Evelyn's name in the paper or hear it spoken on TV. The neighbors knew she was bad news anyway, and they gossiped incessantly about her behind her back.

Evelyn was the town drunk. She was a whore. Pop estimated that she had slept with probably half the men in Pittsburgh (the bottom half, for sure) and whenever he met someone who knew his mother he always felt uncomfortable, a pit gnawing in his stomach out of fear that Evelyn had slept with his new acquaintance. Pop generally assumed that he had brothers and sisters everywhere, little bastard half-siblings – this was a blithe assumption on his part because he had never seen his mother pregnant, or known her to have been pregnant in the past with anyone besides himself.

He had been an accident. Pop learned this from Sugar who informed him that he had been "unintended" and "unplanned," and that he owed his existence to his grandmother, who had talked her daughter out of an abortion. Pop consequently thought of himself as an abortion that lived, a status that he liked better than just being an "accident," which is kind of like being a car wreck or a fall from a ladder. Existentially speaking, being an abortion that lived was better than being an accident because it didn't imply that he had come about by carelessness or mistake, at least not completely.

The exact contours of his accidental beginning were unknown to him. His father, whom Evelyn never married, was some guy named Schadel Sammler whose family hailed from Carrick or Overbrook and like the other Germans who resided there, looked down on the Serbs and Poles who lived in the Heights. That being said, Sammler wasn't any prize. He had a mental disorder and a history of being committed to Western Psych a couple of times, once for cutting his wrists with a kitchen knife and another time for a breakdown he suffered after he found Evelyn in bed with another man. Although he claimed to love her, Sammler eventually decided he just couldn't live with Evelyn. This was after Pop was born. After the breakup (which was preceded by the breakdown), Evelyn and Pop moved in with Sugar and Gran, and Sammler went to live with his parents in Carrick or Overbrook or wherever the hell he was from. Evelyn and Pop would hear about him every once in a while. One time, he was reportedly institutionalized for threatening to jump off a bridge, an incident that tied up traffic for an hour and a half while the police talked him down. Another time, he was found naked on the streets and the cops picked him up for indecent behavior. Eventually he mellowed out on the right anti-depressant drugs, moved out from his parents' house, got himself a job, and even paid Evelyn occasional child support. Then Pop turned 18, and the support checks stopped. Pop lost touch with Sammler after that, and he wasn't sure if he even lived in Pittsburgh anymore.

Pop never really believed that Sammler was his father. According to Sugar, Evelyn was carrying on with three or four other men around the time that Pop was born, and any one of them could have been his dad. There was some Irishman named Murphy who loved his booze and was something of a minor criminal, having been jailed for kiting checks and receiving stolen goods. Murphy once gave Pop a baseball, glove and bat and told him to use them in good health. In addition to Murphy, there was a school teacher who adored Evelyn and always bought her flowers and took her to dinner at expensive places and sometimes made her sigh with genuine emotion, but failed to move her in the bedroom where it really counted. Lastly, there was some guy named Addler who was just using mum for sex, according to Sugar-Pop. (Pop tried to suppress the thought that he could have been conceived by some Jew.)

***

My lawyer, Ronni Silverstein, is Jewish. I saw her a lot before my trial and a couple of times after I came here. She has big horned-rimmed glasses and curly black hair pulled back in a bun, which I think she wears that way to look severe, to help her make her way in a world of male judges, male lawyers, male cops and correction officers without being distracted from her job by sexual innuendo and crude jokes (how's that working for you, Ronni?) Her nose, as you might have expected, is somewhat accentuated. But she has straight white teeth and Jolie lips, the kind you'd like to slip your tongue between, at least you would if you were me.

I always like to see her. It makes the bullshit one has to put up with for a visit here almost seem worthwhile. Before he can see a visitor here, a death row inmate is stripped down and forced to spread his arms and legs and cheeks. The correctional officers inspect every one of his body cavities – his mouth, his armpits, and his asshole – to make sure he isn't hiding drugs or a weapon, anything that could be passed to another inmate in the hall. The same process gets repeated after the visit is over and the inmate is back in his cell. It's all ridiculous, of course. Death row inmates aren't permitted contact visits. They see their visitors through a glass, and there isn't any way in hell that the visitor could pass something to the inmate. Nor is it possible for the inmate to pass something to another inmate as he is escorted down the hall to the no-contact visit booth. His hands and feet are cuffed and chained, and there is a whole bevy of correctional officers escorting him, and never, never in any of my trips outside my cell, have I had a chance to pass even so much as a welcome note to another inmate. It goes without saying that I'm never getting anything in return, not a shiv or a metal kitchen ladle, nothing sharp or edged, not any kind of improvised weapon, nor anything that would get me high either, not an OxyContin tab or any other kind of "cheek" pill, not even just a half a joint of grass.

Ronni has small breasts and the last time she came to see me I asked her if she would press them up against the glass in the visit booth. She clucked her tongue and told me I needed to stay on task. She rambled on about my appeal while I stared at her tits.

After my trial, Ronnie filed post-sentencing motions with the trial court and then took a direct appeal to the state Supreme Court, where my case now sits, and where it will probably sit for the next five years. When my appeal is denied, as I am certain that it will be, Ronni will ask the U.S. Supreme Court to review the case, which it most certainly will decline to do. The next stop in the process is a new appeal under the Post-Conviction Relief Act, which goes first to the trial court then back up to the state Supreme Court. I am guaranteed another few years of breathing while the PCRA appeal runs its course. Then it's federal habeas, which would start at the U.S. District Court level and include all federal constitutional issues from my direct appeal and my post-conviction claims. This phase could take another two to six years, attorney Silverstein patiently explained.

Truth be told, my attorney is more interested in keeping me alive than I am. I think it would be a great burden on her conscience if I were put to death. She certainly isn't representing me for the money. As a public defender, she makes next to nothing, far less than an attorney in private practice, a D.A., or the judge who sentenced me.

I don't really try to understand her motivation. She is a do-gooder, probably a liberal, one of those types that the people I knew growing up really hate, one of those types that most of the people in this country hate. Throw in the fact that she is a Jew (for all I know, she's gay, too), and the hate meter really spikes. I can tell you that it gives me some satisfaction to know that, in certain circles, Ronni Silverstein is more despised than I am.

This small, despised woman is, in all likelihood, the only woman that I will ever get to see in here, the only one I will ever get to spend any time with face-to-face, even if it is with a pane of glass between us. This gives our relationship a special kind of intimacy, even though I know that Ronni Silverstein hasn't the slightest interest in me as a sexual being.

She is one of two reasons why I haven't pulled the plug on my appeal. The first is this book, my lifeline to the future, which, I must confess, sometimes depresses the hell out of me. There are times when I would just as soon forget about Sugar-Pop or Mummy or Marge or Keilah or Ray or any of the other characters I grew up with, as much as I would like to write another word about them. So sometimes that just leaves me with my little Jewish princess. I often think about her while I masturbate, particularly after a visit, when my memory of her face, her breasts, her aura is still fresh, and when the better looking celebrities I see on the TV in my cell fail to get me hard.

That's the price she pays for keeping me alive.

***

Pop was afraid of what Evelyn might say after he got fired. He called KG and they went to Junior Olup's place on the South Side (where they could get in without ID) and drank themselves pissy-assed drunk. Pop spent the night at KG's place, and in the morning, after worshipping the porcelain bowl most of the night, and sipping some black coffee very tentatively when he got up, asked Kenny what he thought he should do.

I don't know Pop, what do you want to do?

Kenny was Pop's friend and all, but he was a complete

idiot, from Pop's point of view.

I don't know, Pop said. I think I'm gonna puke some more. Then when I'm finished, maybe I'll see a recruiter and join the Marines.

That, in fact, was exactly what Pop did.

There were a couple of hurdles he had to clear before he could do it.

The first one, and the one Pop worried about the most, was his amblyopia. He was scared as hell it would keep him out. The recruiter he spoke to said it would ultimately be up to the doctor at the Military Processing Entrance Station, or MEPS, but as long as he didn't want to be a pilot, it shouldn't be a problem. The recruiter, who was a Marine Sergeant, said he had a Corporal in his old unit with lazy eye and he could watch two fields of fire at one time! I just couldn't ask him to use a pair of binoculars, the Sergeant quipped.

Pop also was concerned that the physical part of him below eye level might be a problem, too. To get into the Marines, one has to be able to do three pull-ups, fifty sit-ups and run three miles in less than 28 minutes. The first two of these requirements was no sweat, literally. Pop could do three pull-ups and fifty sit-ups without breaking a sweat. The three mile run, however, was a little more challenging because Pop was a smoker, and, as a consequence, didn't have any wind. Shit, Pop said, when he found himself getting gassed after running for about a minute. I'm going to have to give up cigarettes.

Then there was the mental hurdle. He had to take and pass the Armed Services Vocational Aptitude Battery test and he had to get a GED. The first part of this was easy. Pop aced the ASVAB. He was ready to get his

GED, too, but his recruiter, who was pretty impressed with Pop's ASVAB score, told him he could get his GED after enlisting. What he didn't tell Pop was that it would cost him about eight grand in perks he wouldn't qualify for without a diploma.

So Pop got into the Marines, but he also got the shaft.

A few days before he left for basic training, he called Keilah and asked her if she wanted to go to Paris with him.

He could hear her exhale deeply through the telephone.

Pop, she said, get real, okay?

I mean it, Pop said.

Yeah, right, Keilah said. And how do you plan to support us? Shit, you don't even speak French.

Oh, I speak French all right, Pop thought, remembering the last time he had kissed her. But he didn't say that. Instead he told her that he already had a job.

Pop, she said, you're so full of shit, you know that?

Then he told her that the Paris he was talking about was a place called Parris Island and his new job was to protect the country.

Oh, Pop, Keilah said.

Pop waited for her to say something else, but she didn't. He thought she was crying, but he wasn't sure, and before he could ask her the line went dead, and she didn't pick up when he called her back.

Pop spent the next couple of minutes throwing darts at the board on his wall. He missed, and one of the darts dug into the plaster. Pop pulled it out and jammed it into the bull's eye. Fuck, he said. My life is all fucked up. He was thinking about calling KG and asking him if he wanted to go to Junior Olup's and get pissy-assed drunk again when the telephone rang. It was Keilah and she asked him if he wanted to come over. Sure, Pop said, but what about Marge? She isn't here, Keilah said. She's out for the evening.

Pop lost his virginity that night. Keilah didn't. It was great getting laid, but Pop had assumed Keilah was a virgin and was saving herself for him. Obviously, that wasn't the case, and when he asked her about it, she looked at him funny and told him that it wasn't any of his business. What do you mean? Pop said. I think I have a right to know who you've been screwing. I'm not a whore, Keilah said, brimming with indignation. I'm not saying you are, Pop told her. I just thought, you know, that I would be your first. She looked at him with the greatest annoyance when he said this, her face getting all scrunchy and her eyelashes battering around like she had lost all control of them. Keilah buttoned her blouse and told him he'd better leave. Okay, Pop said. He tried to kiss her flush on the lips one last time before he left, but Keilah turned away from him and jumped up from the bed, and all he got was her fleeting shadow.

***

Shortly after I came here, one of the COs got piqued at me while I was taking my first shower. I had taken a few quick march steps to the shower head, pulled the ring, and wetted my hair. I soaped and rinsed my hair and face and then, holding the bar of soap in my right hand, started to soap and rinse my left arm. The guard was annoyed with my deliberate style of washing. Stop clowning around, he snapped. I tried to explain to him that I was just taking a shower "by the numbers," the way

I had been taught in the Marines. He wanted no part of my explanation, and pulled me away from the shower head, causing me to slip and fall on the tiled floor. Three or four other COs came in to assist the officer who had knocked me down. I was cuffed and manacled, and taken, nude, soaking wet and bleeding, back to my cell.

Showering by the numbers was one of two things that stuck with me after I got out of the Corps. The other was "The Marine Rifle Creed." It stuck with me because (a) it's really cool, and (b) one of my favorite songs, "Crisis" by the Fear Factory, does a riff on it: "Hey, Sergeant do you know who's in command here? Motherfucker! This is my rifle. There are many like this, but this one is mine. …" Plus, I really like that scene from Full Metal Jacket where Gunnery Sergeant Hartman calls the new recruits "pukes" and orders them to sleep with their rifles. "You will give your rifle a girl's name," Sergeant Hartman shouts, "because this is the only pussy you people are going to get!"

***

Pop called his rifle "Kill'ya" in honor of his girlfriend. Pop was issued his M16A2 Service Rifle during Phase One of boot camp, right after finishing "Forming Week," the processing week that every new recruit goes through and during which he gets a buzz cut, does his paperwork, takes his Initial Strength Test and learns to get screamed at and how to scream back ("Sir, Yes, Sir!). Pop didn't actually get to fire his weapon until the seventh week or so of boot camp. Prior to qualifying with the M16A2, Pop learned how to drill with it, how to clean it, how to site it, how to make allowance for distance and windage, and how to "dry-fire" it, snapping the rifle while standing, sitting, kneeling, lying prone and so forth. (His D.I. called the training "dry humping," and Pop concurred that it was the Kama Sutra of rifle positions.)

Rifle training was the only part of boot camp that Pop didn't despise. Pop hated the marching and the drilling, the P.T., or physical training, the screaming and the yelling, the abuse. He hated getting "quarter-decked," or punished by being forced to do extra sets of push-ups, crunches, and side straddle hops or running in place for hours. He especially hated the depersonalizing aspects of boot camp, from the uniformity of the haircuts to the standard issue uniforms, from the insanity of doing every simple, stupid thing "by the numbers" to the inanity of the Corps' vocabulary and language, such as insisting on calling a floor a "deck" or a window a "porthole," (shit, they weren't in the Navy), or requiring a recruit to refer to himself in the third person, and never as "I" (a practice that stuck with him).

If he had thought about it, boot camp was excellent training for jail. In boot camp, they take away your civilian clothes and issue a uniform, one that is only slightly more in vogue than prison stripes. In both places, discipline starts the moment you get off the bus. In prison, as in the Marines, you are told where to stand (and when and where to shit), although SCI-Garrow did not have the equivalent of the Yellow Footprints that are painted on the ground at Parris Island and used to show where (and how) the new recruits are to stand in their first formation.

Weapons training almost made up for all the bullshit. Firing the M16A2 was a thrill, notwithstanding the fact that the rear sight was virtually useless and that the M16A2 didn't really measure up to the Kalashnikov, or so Pop heard (at the time, he didn't own one and had never shot one of the Russian-made or Russian-inspired models.) He had to shoot right-handed because of his amblyopia but he was right hand-dominant anyway: His marksmanship was okay on the known-distance course he trained on, and even better on the field firing range where you had to shoot at moving and multiple targets, and under low-light conditions, and so forth – situations that more closely approximately actual combat, to Pop's mind at least. Hell, he didn't want to be a sharpshooter like Lee Harvey Oswald, who plugged Kennedy in the head from a distance of about 190 yards, or Charles Whitman, who scored 215 out of a possible 250 in long-range shooting and killed 16 people and wounded 32 others from the observation deck of a 307-foot tower on the campus of the University of Texas in Austin in 1966. Both Oswald and Whitman had learned to shoot in the Marines. Whitman also got bayonet training there, which may have come back to him while he was stabbing his wife three times in the heart as she slept and before he commenced his shooting rampage from the tower. (Whitman, by the way, had an IQ of 138, just one point higher than Pop's.)

No, sir, Pop wasn't sharpshooter grade, but he wasn't a complete washout as a marksman. He was just a washout as a Marine. Later, he told everyone he got kicked out of the corps for throwing a punch at his drill sergeant, which wasn't true, but made a better story than the actual facts of the matter, which was that Pop got a psych discharge. The truth of the matter is that he missed Keilah so much that he was thinking about her all the time and not really concentrating on what he was doing and then he kind of broke down one day (actually, a couple of times) and started bawling about how much he missed her in front of his Second Hat, who turned him in and caused him to have to undergo some testing. That's when the Corps found out he had a personality disorder (albeit a "borderline" one) and decided to separate him from its ranks. In the last analysis, Pop was semper fi, just not in the way that he wanted or imagined.

Kill ya

The minute Pop got home from the Marines he looked up personality disorder on Mum's computer. He read that people with personality disorder are often uncertain about their identity (shit, who isn't?), have chronic feelings of emptiness (ditto) and difficulty controlling anger (who doesn't want to blow off a little steam now and then?) They also tend to see things in terms of extremes, such as all good or all bad. Pop, frankly, didn't see how any of that applied to him, or what there was about it that would make him unsuitable for the Corps. He concluded that he had just rubbed somebody the wrong way.

After he had satisfied his curiosity about the Corps' diagnosis of him, Pop called Keilah and asked her if they could get together. Keilah thought he was still on Parris Island, and didn't quite believe that he was home, even after he explained it to her. She wasn't sure it was a good idea to hook up, not yet. But Pop begged and pleaded and finally Keilah relented and said she would drop over.

They talked for a while, and Pop told her he was dishonorably discharged from the Corps for throwing a food tray at a drill instructor. He didn't want to lie to her, but he had already told KG and his mum that this was what had happened. Keilah didn't look pleased hearing what was to become the official story of his separation from the Marines, and Pop wondered if it would have gone over any better with her if he had told her the truth, that he was a psycho. In any event, Keilah got all uptight and prickly with him, and he had to tell her he loved her to cop so much as a feel, and he believed he said "I love you" to her about twelve times before she loosened up and went down on him.

Afterward, she told him that he was still persona non grata with Marge and it would be better if he laid low for a while – no calls to her house when Marge was home and they shouldn't chance getting caught making out on her sofa or even being seen together in the hood. Are we going together or not? Pop said, giving her his best hangdog expression, and she said, yeah, we are, but he could be cool for a change.

The only good thing about the chill (more of a still than a chill, actually) in his relationship with Keilah was that it got him on better terms with his mum. Mum blamed all of his problems on his girlfriend. His getting sacked by Mr. Savage was all her fault, as was his getting thrown out of the Marines. She was the reason he was a head case. Keilah was a little whore who thought she was better than everyone else, just like her mother, Marge. Well, Pop would prove her wrong in time, Evelyn was certain, and in the meantime, she kept out of his way and gave him his space, not getting on him about being a fuck up, or not having a job.

Pop responded by being genuinely industrious. He got up early every day and took his shower by the numbers and did his crunches and sit-ups and side straddle hops, just like he had done in basic training. He even started to run, although he hadn't completely weaned himself from cigarettes. Pop found Sugar-Pop's old barbells in the basement, and started to work out.

He also began to read.

THE POLITICIZATION OF PETER POPOVICH, PART 2

He started with a book he picked up at a gun show in Monroeville that was given to him by some guy who was looking to sell him a handgun, then got all jacked off when he found out Pop was just 18. You can't transfer a handgun to an 18-year-old in Pennsylvania, not even at a gun show, without processing the sale through the County sheriff, which the gun dealer wouldn't do. So Pop didn't get himself a handgun, but he got this book instead.

It was called Unintended Consequences, and it had a picture on its cover of Lady Justice being assaulted by an ATF agent. Lady Justice was scantily clad and wearing a blindfold, and Pop thought the cover was pretty cool. The book began with a couple of short staccato sentences about three military choppers coming over a ridge. They were coming to kill the book's protagonist and hero, an embattled gun owner who just wanted the government to leave him the fuck alone.

Although the book was fiction, it had a lot of shit in it about the history of America's gun laws, which pretty much started under that commie Roosevelt with the passage of the National Firearms Act in 1934. The NFA imposed a $200 tax on shortened shotguns, fully automatic guns, and silencers. According to John Ross, the book's author, it set a legal precedent that would spawn other, even more outrageous infringements on the right to bear arms, metastasizing like a tumor into an ever-widening and more aggressive form of cancer.

Unintended Consequences described the history of this illness, stopping, along the way, to tell the reader what really happened at Ruby Ridge, where the federal government used the alleged sale of two sawed-off shotguns as a pretext to shoot a man's wife in the head and his son in the back, killing them both. The book also set its sights on the siege at Waco, Texas, where the feds turned machine guns and tanks on a group of people and burned eighty-six of them alive because one of them, David Koresh, had allegedly failed to pay the $200 tax.

Pop read the book in fascination and in horror. He could have done without the part about the Warsaw Uprising, which made Jews look like heroes, and was thrown in to equate U.S. gun laws with those the Nazis imposed. He also wasn't sure that the consequences Ross described were all that unintended: Pop was still smarting from his own recent brush with government, where he had been jerked off first by a recruiter who screwed him out of pay and then by some government shrink who was trying to put the kibosh on him for God knows what reason. He was also miffed because he was old enough to join the Marines and train with an M16, but he wasn't old enough to buy himself a pistol.

Pop's immediate reaction to the book (and his

situation) was to go out and buy a shotgun, which he could do without processing the transaction through the Sheriff or waiting until he was 21. He got himself a .12 gauge Mossberg Maverick 88 pump shotgun, which had an 18-1/2 inch barrel and was 39-1/2 inches overall in length. It came equipped with a red-dot site and set Pop back $169.95.

The second thing he did was to continue reading. He read books you couldn't buy at Borders or find at the Carnegie Library, but that were available for download or purchase from the net. He read The Turner Diaries, which starts after the federal government has confiscated all civilian firearms under the Cohen Act and ends with someone flying an airplane into the Pentagon. A copy of The Turner Diaries was found in Timothy McVeigh's car when he got arrested on a traffic stop after bombing the Alfred P. Murrah building in Oklahoma City.

Pop read None Dare Call It Conspiracy, which was about the takeover of the United States by a group of international bankers, like the Rothchilds, who helped to finance both sides of the Civil War. Later, according to the book, the conspiracy was spearheaded by financiers like the Rockefellers, who helped to prop up the Bolsheviks by selling their bonds through the Chase Manhattan Bank and promoted communism as an ideal through their Foundation.

Pop read Henry Ford's The International Jew, which he bought from the website of The National Alliance for $39.45, which was a lot to pay for a book, but was worth it. Ford basically predicted the New World Order long before it happened and his book showed who was behind it. The book showed how the Jews used power and came to exert a vast influence over American life and politics. Ford linked Zionism and Bolshevism, and told how liberalism, which is Bolshevism without the Budyonny caps and hairy Leninesque chins, was the source of most of the problems in the world, corrupting art, music and literature, as well as government. Most Americans knew of Henry Ford as an automaker but didn't know that he was a social thinker, too. Pop heard that Hitler had a copy of The International Jew in his library and that he put a photograph of Ford on the wall in his study so he could look at it from time to time.

Around this time, Pop also started to listen to The Alex Jones Show on the radio and to follow Alex Jones on the web, where he was popularizing his theory of the New World Order and the conspiracy behind it. Like Gary Allen in None Dare Call It Conspiracy, Jones went easy on the Jews, choosing not to blame one group but an ideology or mindset for the takeover of the world by the international banking elite. Later, Pop read somewhere that Jones' wife was Jewish, and he wondered if that was why he pulled his punches or maybe even if Jones himself was part of the conspiracy he was describing. Although Jones may have been suspect, Pop had to admit that he admired his brass, such as when Jones said the Marines were stupid brainwashed punks for allowing themselves to be used as pawns by the New World Order.

Pop also had to admit that his reading raised more questions than it answered. Sometimes he found that he simply didn't know enough. For example, Gary Allen maintained that The Communist Manifesto was secretly written by Adam Weishaupt, founder of the Bavarian Illuminati, and not by Karl Marx, who just happened to sign his name to it. Later, Pop read that Weishaupt killed George Washington and took his place as the first president of the United States, and that all the portraits of Washington that you see, like those in the National Gallery or the face on the one dollar bill, are really of Weishaupt. Pop didn't know if that was true, but the story was so breathtakingly beautiful he wanted to believe it.

When he wasn't reading, or working out, Pop spent most of his time thinking about Keilah. He basically just didn't understand her. And their relationship was kind of going in reverse – from full sex to oral to a hand job on the city steps in back of his house every now and then. She wouldn't invite him over to her place, even at times when he knew Marge wouldn't be there. And she wasn't keen on spending time at his place either. Pop asked her if it was because of his mum, but Evelyn wasn't home much anymore (she had a new beau, another Ray, named Frank), and Keilah said, no that wasn't it.

What is it? he asked her, but she just shrugged her shoulders.

He thought, maybe, it had something to do with the shotgun and the books he had been reading, so he asked her if that was it, and she told him he could read whatever he wanted; in fact, she was glad he was reading something and maybe someday it would be Leo Tolstoy instead of Andrew Macdonald. She allowed that the shotgun made her feel somewhat uncomfortable, those were her words.

The next time he saw her he told her she didn't have to worry about the shotgun anymore. He had removed it.

She checked. Sure enough, it wasn't in the closet in

his room where he had been keeping it.

Where'd you put it? she asked.

Somewhere safe.

Won't you tell me?

Well, why won't you tell me a couple of things first? Pop said. Then he tried to get her to open up about her sex life, who she had lost her virginity to, when and where it had happened, whether it was before or after Pop came on the scene. All Keilah would tell him was, Pop, that's none of your business. It is my business if you were screwing someone at the same time you were screwing me, Pop told her. Did you see anyone else in the room with us when we were having sex? she asked. That's not what I meant, Pop said. I was asking whether you were sleeping with someone around the same time you were sleeping with me? Like, for example, are you sleeping with anyone else now? Right now? she asked. No, I don't mean right now, Pop said with rising agitation. You know what I mean.

But she didn't know, or at least she wasn't saying. Finally, out of exasperation, Pop told her that he had taken the shotgun and buried it in the park near his house.

She looked at him as if he were a werewolf or some other kind of creature that only came out when the moon was full. All I know, Keilah told him, is that we're not married, we're not engaged to be married, we're not even planning to be married, and Christ, I'd like to finish school before I make any other major plans in my life.

In other words, this isn't an exclusive relationship, Pop said. So I can just fuck off?

Suit yourself, Keilah told him.

Who are you sleeping with? he asked her.

Screw yourself, she said.

Does he give you orgasms?

Keilah looked at him with a scowl.

Do I give you orgasms? Pop asked her.

Look, Keilah said, I think it's time we both went home.

***

The next time he saw her, he tried to avoid the subject of sex entirely. They were sitting at the kitchen table at his mum's house. (His mum was at the Lyceum, drinking her morning beer with Frank.) I registered to vote, he announced proudly.

Yeah, great, she said. It's about time. You could have registered in May when you turned 18.

Well, I did it now so I can vote in the 2004 election for Bush.

You're not serious, are you? Keilah said.

Damn straight.

You registered Republican?

Yep-per.

And you're going to vote for Bush?

That's right.

You know he's a goddamn idiot, Keilah said.

Yeah, but Kerry's queer.

What makes you think so?

I saw a picture of him windsurfing.

Jesus Christ, Pop.

He looked pretty gay to me. Plus his wife's butch.

Keilah swiped a strand of her hair away from her eyes, and squinted at him. You're just playing with me, right?

Nope.

You really think Kerry's gay?

A real faggot, Pop spat. F-A-G-G-O-T.

I guess you would know.

What's that supposed to mean?

It means you're the expert on homosexuals, I suppose. Keilah got up from the table and started to put on her jacket. Takes one to know one I guess.

She had one arm in a sleeve and was just starting to put in the other one when Pop smacked her in the face. Blood spurted from her nose onto her blouse. What the hell did you do that for? Keilah asked in shock.

Pop grabbed her by the hair and yanked her toward him. Don't talk to me like that ever again, you hear? Then he released her hair and pushed her away from him as hard as he could. She banged up against the refrigerator with her right shoulder. Keilah pulled her jacket up over her blouse and looked at him in horror. Her eyes were filling with tears as she raced out the door.

Fucking cunt, Pop said to her fleeing back.

***

A few hours later, a squad car pulled up in front of Pop's house. Pop cringed when he saw it, and, for a moment, he wished he had buried his Maverick in the yard, where he could get to it quicker. Then he thought about running away, but the officer had already seen him, so Pop decided to play it cool. He sauntered over to the police car and asked the officer if he could be of any help.

The officer asked him if he was Peter Popovich, and when he said he was, the officer served him with a copy of Keilah's Petition for Protection from Abuse. He also handed Pop a Temporary Order barring Pop from going to Keilah's house until a hearing was held on the Petition. The deputy told him he had to show up for the hearing or the State Police would be out to arrest him. Stay away from her in the meantime, the officer said.

After the officer left, Pop stood in the yard and read the Petition to himself. It didn't say anything about Pop smacking Keilah in the nose. It just said he had pulled her hair and called her names. It also said that Pop had threatened her if he caught her with other men. Pop didn't remember saying it exactly that way, but he guessed it captured the drift, or tenor, of what he meant.

Threatened her with what?

One of the paragraphs mentioned the gun he had buried in the park. The Petition didn't say he had threatened her with the gun, but Pop suddenly saw things from Keilah's point of view. Maybe secrets should stay secret after all, Pop said to himself. Keilah's sex life was her fucking business (no pun intended), and his shotgun was his goddamn business, and he really wished he hadn't said anything about it to her at all. He wished he had kept his effin' mouth shut. In the future, he promised himself, he would be more discreet.

***

At the hearing, the judge extended the PFA for 18 months. Eighteen fucking months! Pop just couldn't imagine going that long before he could see Keilah again. Then the thought occurred to him that she might never want to see him again, and he felt like his life was over.

After the hearing, Pop went home and got a shovel and went to the park and dug up his Maverick. Then he took it back to his room and cleaned and oiled it. He put a shell in the chamber, and put the stock to the floor and the barrel in his mouth, like he was giving it a blow job. He wondered if this was the right way to do it. He didn't know. Pop had heard that Kurt Cobain held his shotgun upside down with the trigger and the trigger guard pointing up when he shot himself. Pop took his mouth off the barrel, which tasted metallic, and spat. He picked the gun up and laid it on his bed where he could look at it while he sat on a chair in a corner of his room. There wasn't any way to do it that wouldn't make a mess and freak out mum, he figured. He worried that he might chicken out at the last moment and flinch and blow his fucking face off instead of blowing his head apart. Cobain had killed himself with a Remington, and Hemingway, he had read, with a Boss. Pop wondered how many people had committed suicide with a Maverick.

Pop stared at the shotgun on the bed for about half an hour. He smoked a half a pack of cigarettes in that period, lighting one right after another, letting the newly lit one dangle from his lips while he was stubbing out the last.

Finally, Pop decided that if he were going to kill himself he should do it in front of Keilah.

***

The suicide rate is nine times higher in prisons and jails than it is outside. Although most suicides in the United States kill themselves with a gun, hanging is the preferred method in prison. Over 80 percent of prison suicides are completed by hanging, which can be accomplished while kneeling, sitting, standing, or even lying down. Methods of hanging include fastening a bed sheet, shoelace, belt, sock, or elastic waist band to a window crank, air duct vent, handrail, bedrail, cell bar or higher points, such as a light fixture or a shower head. Since it only takes 2 kilograms (4.409 pounds) of pressure on the neck to cut off blood flow to the brain, hanging can be completed in practically no time. Death occurs in five to seven minutes, but permanent brain damage can result in as little as three.

The guy who had this cell before me hanged himself. His name was Billy Till and he was found dead one day at about 6:15 in the morning. I'm not exactly sure how he did it, and no one here is inclined to tell me. A book in the prison library says that jail suicides can be prevented by designing air vents with holes that are too small to thread a sheet through, eliminating exposed pipes, hinges and knobs, and using break-away shower heads.

Frequent monitoring of inmates can also be effective in reducing prison suicides, although the book acknowledges that staffing issues may impose limits on the number of cell checks and that the installation of surveillance cameras may raise privacy and civil rights concerns. (Tell that to the warden!) In the last analysis, and I am quoting here, it comes down to the human element, who is looking and who cares.

Billy Till had served as the prison librarian. He had been on death row for 23 years.

**

Pop waited until it was dark before he went to Keilah's. He took the old Buick that Pop had given to Evelyn, who couldn't drive it because she had her license taken away after her third DUI. Pop got the engine to turn over, but the old Buick choked and coughed and sputtered and it took a while before he was confident that it wouldn't die on him. He gassed it up at the local BP and drove around for a while before heading off to his destination. Pop turned the headlights off the moment he turned onto Keilah's street, and struck the curb hard as he parked in front of her house, causing him to worry that he had blown out a tire. He tried inspecting it in the dark, and the tire looked fine, as far as he could tell.

The lights were out in Keilah's house and he couldn't tell if she had gone to bed, or just wasn't home. Pop walked the perimeter of her property, the Maverick in his hands. He felt like he was on guard duty. It was a clear night, unusual for Pittsburgh, with the stars bright in the sky. For some reason, they reminded him of overhanging fruit, and he wanted to reach out and pick them. Pop inhaled the crisp night air deep into his lungs.

Pop listened for sounds from Keilah's house, but he couldn't hear any. Maybe she and Marge had decided to spend the night with a relative. He thought about prying open a window and going inside to look, to see if they were sleeping in their beds or were really gone, but thought better of it, and went to sit in his car for a while. He fell asleep with the Maverick in his lap.

The next morning, Pop drove to the Waterworks and staked out the Eat'n Park, where Keilah worked as a waitress. He didn't know when her shift was supposed to start, and he didn't want to arouse the suspicions of any bystanders by being seen with the Maverick in his hands. He put the shotgun in his trunk, and went into the Eat'n Park and got himself a cup of coffee and a Smiley cookie. No Keilah. He got himself a free refill, drank it, and went back outside and waited in his car. He had his hands on the wheel, and kept the motor running while he waited.

Close to noon, he saw her scurry into the Eat'n Park with her waitress uniform on, the brown skirt and mini tie hanging over a white blouse, her blue apron tied in a pretty bow. She looked swell, really swell, a sight for sore eyes, Pop thought. He waited a minute or two before he walked into the Eat'n Park, leaving the Maverick in his trunk. He walked past the hostess and into the main dining room. Keilah was waiting on a couple of guys in paint caps sitting in a booth. Pop walked toward her and, the minute he had her attention, dropped down on a knee and reached for her hand. Will you marry me? he asked her.

Keilah kept her hands in her apron. He could hear her take a breath, a deep one, the way one does when surprise catches in the throat like a big lump of something bad. She put one of her hands over her heart, and exhaled slowly. You're not supposed to be here, Pop, she told him.

Then a manager came up, and one of the paint guys asked her if Pop was bothering her, and he heard someone say, call 9-1-1. Pop looked into Keilah's eyes and pleaded with her silently. Can't we just forget about it? Can't we erase the past and rewind the tape and start all over? That's what his eyes said, but she wasn't listening, and Pop figured he better get the hell out of there before the cops arrived.

An hour later, he walked into the Zone 3 station on the South Side and turned himself in. They charged him with indirect criminal contempt for violating the PFA, and took him to the Allegheny County jail. He got processed and was taken to District Court next door, where he was arraigned and got released on his own recognizance, without having to post bond. A hearing got scheduled, but he didn't have to go, because Keilah didn't press charges or whatever. It didn't matter. He wasn't going to bother her again. A few days later, he boarded a Greyhound bus to Florida. They didn't say goodbye, and he never saw her in person again, although she did have an altercation with his mother later, and he talked to her on the phone for a while on the morning of his last real day in this world.

Ghost

The first thing Pop did when he got to Florida was to stop at Juno Beach and watch the waves roll in. He was there at daybreak, watching the sun rise from the sea like Poseidon's crown, streamers of gold and yellow breaking through the clouds. He put a blanket down on the sand, just past the tidemark, and set his pocket AM/FM radio on it, together with his shoes, and rolled up his trousers and walked out on the beach. He felt like he was in a postcard; it was that perfect. Pop decided he needed to get a picture to send back home, and fished his cell phone out of the button-down pocket in his denim shirt, and moved back, past the tidemark, and caught a huge swell in the distance, and clicked. He got a great picture of it as it broke, and then he watched the foam wave wash up on the beach, over the tidemark, soaking his blanket, right up to his feet.

Pop spent the next couple of days there, hanging around the pier (it cost a dollar), and then he went into nearby Palm Glades to find a job and a place to stay.

He found an ad in the paper for a vacancy and went out to look at it right away. Pop told the woman who was renting it that he was studying to be a dentist at the Lincoln College of Technology in West Palm (he had one of the school's brochures tucked into his shirt pocket, where she could see it), and she took pity on him and waived the two-month security deposit she had wanted. The unit was in the back of her house, but had a separate entrance, and the only thing bad about it was that it didn't have an internet connection. Pop's landlord's name was Cohen, but she didn't look Jewish. Pop thought she looked hot. She had long brown hair that reminded him of Keilah's, and a cute little butt. She was too old for him, of course (Pop figured she was in her 30's, trending north), and he believed in the maxim his grand pop had taught him, about not shitting where you eat (or, in this case, slept.) Still, it was nice to flirt with a woman for a change, and not have someone call the cops on you.

The job was a harder nut to crack. Pop studied the classifieds in the paper every day, and blanketed Palm Glades with applications, but didn't have any success until he discovered the public computers at the library and logged on to monster and got a lead on a job as a glazier in Boynton Beach. He called the guy on the phone and he was interested. It sounded like a lot of hard work. He would be installing new and replacement doors and windows, which would mean a lot of lifting, but Pop liked the idea of using power tools and he could picture himself handling glass without breaking it (although he wondered what mum would think of that.) The job meant that he would have to get a car, but he was quickly discovering that you couldn't get around Palm Glades or anywhere else in southern Florida without a vehicle of your own. (Unlike Pittsburgh, there weren't sidewalks everywhere, and the public transportation system sucked.)

Pop got himself a used Ford F-150 pickup truck, spending the last of the money he had earned in the Marines on a down payment. The truck was red, and Pop was leery of buying it because he had heard that red cars are ticketed for speeding more than any other cars. He also heard that they were stolen more frequently than other vehicles, but the salesmen who sold the F-150 to him told him that was bull. It didn't matter, because Pop needed a car and didn't really have time to shop around.

The job was okay. His crew mostly did replacement windows, and once Pop learned how to measure and fit the units in place, making sure they were level and secure and sealed up weather tight, he kind of got the hang of it. His boss wasn't an asshole like Mr. Savage, but he worked the crew hard and there wasn't any time to screw around. Pop hooked up with a guy on the crew who he had a couple of beers with and who turned him on to Stormtroop, which was an internet forum and was one of the things that had attracted Pop to Palm Glades in the first place.

Stormtroop was a white power web site. Anti-black. Anti-Jew. It was one of those places where you could get the news without all the bullshit of the mainstream media and find out what was really happening in America. It was run by some guy out of his home in Palm Glades. The guy had been a former Grand Dragon in the Ku Klux Klan, or something like that, and Pop thought about knocking on his door, but he wasn't sure that would be cool. (He also was a little afraid that he might be shot, being new to the neighborhood and from the north and all.) So instead, he just logged on to Stormtroop as often as he could, using one of the computers in the Palm Glades public library. Pop posted one of the pictures he had taken on Juno beach, and he made a comment or two about how white women were more attractive than women of all other races, especially the black race (he didn't like big lips and wiggly hips any more than he liked kinky hair), but mostly he was just a lurker.

One of the things Pop liked about Palm Glades was that it was virtually all white and you didn't see blacks or Asians on the streets, or if you did they really stood out, allowing you plenty of time to get on over to the other side. It kind of made sense, Pop thought, that Palm Glades was the capital of the Stormtroop nation. Another thing Pop liked was that there were more young people, a lot more, than there were in Pittsburgh, and the ratio of women to men was a whole lot better, too.

That being said, his social life sucked. The problem with being a white supremacist in America was that there weren't a lot of places where you could meet single white chicks to date, particularly now that the movement had gone on line and people didn't hold Ku Klux Klan meetings anymore. (He figured it would be kind of like searching for Barbie in a burka anyway – you'd have to get her home and get the sheet off before you'd know who you were getting beneath the sheets with, so to speak). And as much as he liked Stormtroop, it wasn't a dating site, or even a social networking site, and it didn't help to dispel his sense of isolation on any of the important fronts of his life, other than the political.

Dan, the guy he had an occasional beer with, suggested he find a hooker and get himself laid. Pop didn't think

West Palm Beach was a mecca of prostitution, but he figured there were whores everywhere (exactly where, Dan couldn't say) so he drove one night down Dixie Highway to take a look around. He passed a rock bar and a night club and a steak house before he saw a scantily dressed blonde woman with nice legs on the corner of Broadway and Dixie. Pop though she might be soliciting, but when he drove back around the block to check her out, he saw a cop car on the corner, and two police officers were cuffing a Mexican and putting him into the back seat of the car. It spooked Pop, and he went home. The next day, he saw something on WPBF 25 about a prostitution sting in West Palm, and he figured he was lucky not to have been arrested.

All this led Pop to get reacquainted with his hand. He didn't have internet in his apartment, and was afraid to troll the web for porn at the public library (he thought he was pushing it just logging on to Stormtroop). He found an adult superstore in Riviera Beach, which was far enough away from Palm Glades that he didn't think anyone would recognize him there (not that anyone knew him anyway). It felt kind of creepy, a little faggy, and he was afraid to view a movie there, but he bought himself a couple of magazines – Celebrity Skin, Cheri and Private (he picked up a copy of Asian Babes but put it back in the rack).

Pop settled in to his new life in Palm Glades. He kept in touch with KG by phone, and every once in a while he would get a call from Evelyn. Mish yah and love yah, she slobbered through the phone, the slavering tone of her speech indicating that she was drunk. (Evelyn never said "I love you" to Pop when she was sober, and, in truth, he would have preferred that she never said it at all. Pop would rather have Evelyn call him a cocksucker than for her to say she loved him. In any event, her "love yah" outbursts only marked a temporary phase in her transition or progression from the drunk to very drunk stage. Pop knew, whenever he talked to her, that the coarser language, the nastier speech, the attack invectives were only another drink or two away.)

Pop spent the winter in Palm Glades, and didn't miss the Pittsburgh snows, and thought maybe he could live here all year round. He also felt he was closer to the center of the political universe – it was here, in Florida, after all, that Al Gore got his ass handed to him in 2000 (even though the Democrats tried to steal it in the recount). Although Palm Beach County, which trended heavily Democratic, gave Kerry big numbers, just like it did for Gore, the 2004 election wasn't razor close, and Pop was happy to be comfortably on the winning side. The night of the election, he thought about calling Keilah after the results were in and telling her he told her so, but he didn't. He just sat in his room and gloated instead.

Pop thought about celebrating Bush's victory by buying himself a handgun. The problem was Florida law. Florida law prohibited the sale of a handgun by a licensed dealer to anyone under 21. Pop thought about buying a rifle or another shotgun instead. (He had left his Maverick in the trunk of his grand pop's Buick and didn't have any weapon in Florida at all.) Getting a rifle or a shotgun was perfectly legal under Florida law. He didn't know why the law discriminated against handguns (and persons under 21) and was lamenting his situation to the guy next door at a block party, when his neighbor asked him if he had any interest in a Bersa Thunder .380 semi-auto. Hell, yeah, Pop said. C'mon, Dale said, let me show it to you. They went across the street to Dale's house and into his garage.

The Bersa was a sweet piece. It had a satin nickel finish and a light aluminum alloy frame. It weighed about 20 ounces. The handgun was equipped with a hammer-drop thumb safety (plus a magazine safety, too) and a long double-action trigger pull with a straight-in feed angle for the magazine. It felt great in Pop's hand.

Two fifty and it's yours, Dale said. It's a great concealed carry piece – a .380 in the pocket is better than a .45 in the truck -- but you can't carry it outside until you're 21 if I sell it to you, agreed?

Agreed, Pop said.

The first thing Pop did after he bought the Bersa was to take it home and take a picture of it on his cell phone. The next day, he uploaded the photo to a Stormtroop forum. The reaction was mostly favorable. Someone told him it was strictly a backup gun IMO because of its low capacity (7 to ten shot magazine) and minimal caliber. Pop repeated Dale's refrain in his head about the .380 in the pocket when he read that. Someone else said it was an ideal weapon for someone with small hands, which kind of honked Pop off.

Pop had some swagger in his step after he bought the handgun. He kept his word to Dale and didn't pack when he left the house, but he imagined walking around with the Bersa tucked under his waist band in a holster and it gave him a whole new feeling of invulnerability. He was feeling so good about himself that he started working out again, and after a few weeks of this, he was starting to show the benefits.

One day, he saw Kathy Cohen mowing the yard, and he offered to do it for her. It was a hot and sticky day and he took his shirt off while he was riding around in her John Deere. Kathy came out and offered him a Papa's Porter microbrew, which was named for Hemingway and tasted a whole lot better than the Iron City he used to drink back home. Sweat was glistening off his chest, and he was pretty sure Kathy was checking out his pecs when she handed him the beer. He wondered if there was any other part of him she might be interested in. Hell, despite her age she was a good-looking woman, and he was wondering if maybe Sugar Pop was mistaken about this not shitting where you eat thing.

He asked Dale about her one evening while they were driving to a local shooting range. Dale didn't know much about her history, or even whether she was single or divorced. He had talked to her at block parties and thought she was nice, but couldn't say what kind of work she did (he thought she did something in West Palm) or even if she was employed at all.

Pop worked 8 to 4 all week, and sometimes on Saturday, so he didn't know if Kathy was around during the day throughout the week. He didn't see her much in the weekday evenings but would sometimes see her on the weekends. He tried to think of things that he could offer to do to help her out. He cut her grass for her a couple of times. Once he saw her on a ladder changing a light fixture over the garage. She was wearing a tight bodice and a pair of tight shorts, and she stretched her calf muscles as she reached to change the bulb. Doesn't that just beat all hell, Pop thought. But he was so entranced by her on the ladder that he forgot to offer any help.

Pop wondered what it would be like to fuck an older woman. Keilah had been a silent lover. Pop wondered if Kathy Cohen would be more vocal. He wondered if she would squirt.

One Friday evening, he noticed a black Lexus in the driveway. He was checking it out (it had a faded blue Kerry-Edwards bumper sticker on it) when Kathy invited him in for a beer and introduced him to this guy named David. He had gray speckled in his beard and was definitely too old for her. Kathy said he was a veterinary doctor, not a regular vet per se, but some kind of specialist, like a cat or dog oncologist. David said he heard Pop was from Pittsburgh. I guess you're a big Steelers fan? he asked.

No, not really, Pop told him.

Oh yeah, why is that?

Pop asked him if he knew what the initials N.F.L. stood for.

The National Football League?

The Negro Football League, Pop told him.

Pop could tell David didn't think that was very funny, so he tried to change the conversation and said he was a Penguins fan. I really like this kid from Quebec they got in the July '05 draft, Pop said. Name of Sidney Crosby. But David didn't know who Sidney Crosby was.

The Lexus was back in the driveway the next Friday, and the Friday and Saturday after that. Pop thought he heard them making love through the walls. And yes, he had been right, his landlord was very vocal. But it didn't get him excited. It made him angry.

The next morning when he went out for a run, he

saw David changing a tire on the Lexus in the driveway. Musta picked up a nail, he muttered. Yeah, Pop told him, you have to be careful where you park around here.

He wanted to tell him you have to be careful where you're sticking it, too, but he just sneered at David as he bounded past him.

A couple of days after that Pop came home and found Kathy playing with a puppy, a white German shepherd, in the yard. The puppy was adorable. Just a couple of months old, it had upright ears and a low set tail that it carried in a slight curve like a saber. It had a pure white coat, of course. A Berger Blanc Suisse, Kathy called it. He asked her if the puppy had a name, and she told him she was going to call her Ghost. Pop thought that sounded stupid. Why not White Fang or Blizzard, or, if you want to stick with the Ghost theme, Hewie after the white German shepherd in the survival video horror game, Haunting Ground?

Thanks very much, Kathy said. But I think I'll just stick with Ghost.

Kathy's veterinarian friend had given her the puppy as a gift. One night on the patio over beers David expounded on the significance of the puppy's breed to Pop. He told Pop that the German shepherd was a breed of dog that originated in Germany around the turn of the last century. After they came to power, the Nazis became particularly fond of the breed, and Adolph Hitler even kept one as a pet, a black-and-brown colored bitch named Blondi, who was given to him by Martin Bohrman. The Fuhrer loved the dog so much he allowed it to sleep with him in his bed. Hitler took Blondi with him to the Fuhrerbunker under the Reich Chancellery during his final days. This turned out to be the dog's undoing. After Hitler learned that Mussolini and his mistress had been shot to death by Italian partisans, who strung their corpses upside down in a village square, he decided that he would not be taken alive. Hitler fretted that the cyanide capsules Himmler had given him might not do the trick, so he asked his doctor to test one on Blondi. The dog died, and Hitler became inconsolably grief-stricken over the loss of Blondi in his final hours.

The thing is, David said, that the white shepherd was regarded as somewhat of an aberration by the Nazis, a genetic mistake, and breeders of the standard colored German shepherds were instructed to drown any whites that were born in their litters. The Nazi antipathy toward the white German shepherd was so great that whites were disqualified from the breed standard after the Nazis took over the German Shepherd Breed Club of Germany. If it were up to the Nazis, David said, dogs like Ghost would have been expunged from the face of the earth. So, David said, as he patted Ghost on the head, she is one side-benefit of our winning the war.

Pop wasn't at all sure that David was right about what he was telling him; in fact, it seemed counterintuitive to Pop. One would think that the Nazis would have celebrated an all-white dog, for Christ's sake. Factor in the consideration that David (most assuredly) was a Jew, and his story became a patently self-serving one, a way to have a really cool looking dog and make believe you were trashing white supremacists in some good-liberal-commie-socialist act of political correctness.

Consequently, Pop went on Stormtroop and posted a query about the white German shepherd breed and got an answer, although it wasn't the one he expected, and it made him hate David all the more.

After that, Pop went through several more nights of wall-banging from David and Kathy. He really couldn't believe that she would allow this guy to touch her, let alone fuck her. But it went on like that all through the fall and winter and into the spring.

In late February, Kathy knocked on his door. She had a glass of wine in her hand and looked a little tipsy. Pop looked behind her but he didn't see David.

What's up? he asked.

Kathy told him that she and David were going away for a couple of days, and she just wanted to give him, you know, the heads up. Would he mind keeping watch over the place while they were away?

Sure thing, Pop said. Where ya goin'?

We're going to Key West.

Pop's face broadened into a smile. You're going on Spring Break, that's what your doin'.

No, no, Kathy told him, her breasts straining against her halter top. That's Fort Lauderdale. We're going to Key West.

Yeah, well, wherever you're going I expect to see you soon in one of those Girls Gone Wild videos.

You think so? Kathy said, exhaling Chardonnay.

Yeah, I think so. You're sure to make the Best of Spring Break edition.

Kathy put one arm up against the doorframe to steady herself, which brought her within arm's reach of Pop. He was about to take her in his arms and hug her, too, when David came padding up behind her.

Where'd you go, babe? he asked. And just like that

Kathy was beyond his reach.

Just letting Pop here know we're leaving for vacation next week, Kathy said as she turned to face David. Asked him to keep watch over the place while we're gone.

I'll look after Ghost, too, Pop blurted out.

No, no, you don't have to do that, David said. We were going to kennel her.

No need to do that, Pop said. Look, this is her home, right? Let her stay and I'll look after her. You can show me where her food is and all and I'll take her outside to do her business. Every day and every night. I promise.

David and Kathy thought that sounded grand.

They left on a Thursday. Pop did what he said and fed and walked Ghost after he got home from work. He got up early on Friday, and had Ghost trail beside him while he ran, and he made sure she did her business after work and before he went to bed. On Saturday, Pop put Ghost in his pickup and drove to Lake Peel. He heard the beach was fairly decent there, and he wanted to check it out. He thought Ghost might like to play in the water, too.

As he drove past the boating area, the first thing he noticed was the signs. There were all kind of signs put up warning about the presence of alligators in the lake. "Caution, Cuidado," the signs read. "Alligators have been seen around Lake Peel. State law prohibits feeding, killing, molesting or attempting to move an alligator."

Oh wow, Pop said aloud. Then he remembered seeing something on the TV about a mammoth alligator that had been photographed in the lake. Some guys in a trauma helicopter that had been flying over the lake had snapped a photograph of the alligator in the water. It was close to 25-feet long and had an animal, a deer maybe or a small dog perhaps, in its jaws as it swam.

Nothing for you and I to worry about, Pop said to Ghost, as he tapped the Bersa under his waistband. If we run into trouble, I'm ready for it.

Pop parked in a secluded area near the water, and they got out and Pop let Ghost run. Here, Ghost, he said, picking up a stick and flinging it from the shore. The stick plopped in the water and floated. C'mon, Ghost, Pop said to the dog. Go fetch it.

Ghost looked at Pop like he was crazy.

C'mon, it's fun, Pop said. He found another stick and tossed it from the shore. Ghost sat on her haunches and panted.

Look at this, Pop said, taking off his shoes and socks. He rolled his trousers about midway up his calf. He walked out over the sand, taking care not to cut his feet on some rocks that were jutting out in his path. Pop scanned the waters of Lake Peel. He didn't see any waves or swells. It was a quiet, virtually windless, day and the lake was pretty calm. He did see an empty Wendy's 42-ounce Super-Size Coca-Cola cup floating just off shore, its lazy progress downstream impeded by a couple of algae-covered logs, but there was nothing in his line of vision that looked anything at all like the snapping head of a Florida gator. Absolutely nothing at all. Of course, Pop had never actually seen a gator. He had seen a croc or two on the Steve Irwin series, The Crocodile Hunter, but he had never seen a gator in real life, except perhaps for a baby one at the Pittsburgh Zoo, where Sugar Pop had taken him when he was a kid. He didn't remember much about the zoo, except the smell of elephants and peanuts and quarter-pound hot dogs sizzling on a grill at the Safari

Village Restaurant, where they ate. He couldn't even say for certain that they had any alligators at the Pittsburgh Zoo at the time he was there. He was certain, however, that he would recognize an alligator if he saw one. Pop ran into the lake and kicked up his feet, splashing the water all around him. Wheeeee, he said to Ghost. Look how much fun I'm having.

The dog practically yawned.

Pop was starting to understand why Hitler didn't like this breed of dog. The trick he guessed, quoting somebody (he didn't know who), was who was to be master, him or the dog. Pop looked at Ghost very sternly. Come here, he said. The dog looked back at him very quizzically. Pop kicked around in the water again, until his pants were soaking wet. Wheeee, he shouted, hollering up a storm. C'mon, Ghost, he screamed at the dog. C'mon, girl, come here!

The dog lifted up her leg and started to lick herself.

Pop took the Bersa out of his waistband and fired a shot that struck the ground a foot and a half or so from the dog.

Ghost took off running.

Aw, fuck, Pop said, tucking the gun back in his waistband. Aw, fuck. He got out on the shore and retrieved his shoes and socks. He put them on and walked up and down the shoreline looking for the dog.

No luck.

Ghost! Pop screamed at the top of his lungs. Come here, girl!

Pop ran up and down the shoreline for a while looking for the dog. Finally, after he felt completed drained and spent from all the walking and running, he went back to his truck. He sat in the pickup for a while wondering what he should do. Then he put the Ford in gear and drove around, looking for Ghost some more. He saw some guy with a couple of kids and asked him if he had seen a dog, a cute white one, German shepherd, you know what I mean? The guy couldn't help him.

Pop decided to drive back to the beach, and search on foot all over again. He had a little trouble finding the place where they had been. He made a couple of wrong turns, and had some trouble retracing his steps. Pop felt really turned around. Finally, he found the secluded spot near the water where he had let Ghost out to run. At least he thought the place looked familiar. He parked the pickup in the same spot (or so he thought) it had been in before, and walked down to the place where he had last seen Ghost. He looked up and down the shoreline. Then he sat down and put his head in his hands and just waited there and listened, hoping to hear Ghost bark.

It was staring to get dark. The sun was squatting on the horizon, like an egg, and it began to flatten and spread out like someone had cracked it and was frying it up in a pan. Pop thought he could feel steam rising. His vision got all squiggly in the dusk, and he wasn't sure he could see Ghost if she came panting right up in front of him. He wondered when the park was supposed to close. Pop looked impatiently at his watch. He wondered how long he could stay out here all by himself. He had read that alligators usually hunt at dusk or night by stalking their prey on shore, and he didn't want to be dinner for some reptile. He had the Bersa, but it wouldn't be much use to him in the dark.

Pop looked up and down the shoreline one last time.

Christ, it was really getting hazy. Pop tried to spot the Coca-Cola cup that had been floating in the water not too far from where he stood, but he couldn't find it. He squinted hard at the shoreline. He saw one algae-covered log where he was sure that there had been two before.

Holy fuck, Pop said.

He turned and made his way back toward his truck, moving as quickly as he could and cursing himself for not bringing a flashlight. In his mind's eye, he shone a light down at the water's edge and saw the red eye of an alligator staring back. Holy fuck, Pop said, tripping over an untied shoelace, and scraping his knee against a rock. He could feel blood dripping down his leg as he climbed up the embankment to the car. He wondered if a gator could smell it. When he got near the car he looked back down at the water again. He tried to make out the log in the water, the algae-covered one that marked the spot where he had last seen Ghost, but it was too dark now to see anything.

Pop got in the pickup, closing the door quickly, and went home. He figured he would drive back up to the Lake on Sunday and look for Ghost again. Shit, maybe they had a Lost and Found for stupid fucking pets.

About eleven o'clock that evening, Pop heard someone knocking at his door. It was Kathy. He was surprised to see her. He hadn't expected her back for several more days.

She looked like hell. She told him that her Key West vacation had been a bust. David and she had too many Papa Dobles at Captain Tony's Saloon, a bar with a tree growing through its roof that Hemingway had frequented in the 1930's. (It appears as Freddy's Bar in the novel, To

Have and Have Not). Anyway, she didn't think David, who had spent the evening stroking his beard and making eyes at every woman in the place, was in any condition to drive. So she got behind the wheel herself. She didn't get too far before she got stopped by the Key West Police, who arrested her for driving under the influence. At the station, she got booked and they took a mug shot, which was the worst of it, because she really looked like shit. David, who was sitting there all Hemingway-like in his panama hat, island shirt and cargo shorts, though it was a hoot.

Anyway, Kathy said, I can tell you more about it in the morning. Right now, I'd just like to get my dog.

Pop could feel his mind turning like tumblers in a lock. What do you mean? he asked her.

Ghost. I've come to take Ghost home.

She's not with you? Pop asked her.

Of course, she's not with me, Kathy said testily. Why do you think I'm here?

I fed her and walked her and left her in your house. She's not with me.

You're kidding.

You're sure she's not there?

Yes. No. David, she called to her boyfriend, Do you see Ghost anywhere?

The three of them spent the next half hour looking everywhere for the dog. Finally, Pop said, he didn't understand it. He let her out so she could do her business, and remembered distinctly putting the dog back in the house. Maybe she got out when they came home, Kathy and David being tired out from their trip, and maybe not paying attention, and all. Pop allowed that after he left Ghost he had stood out in the yard for a couple of minutes smoking a cigarette – he knew how much they disapproved of him smoking in the apartment – and it's possible that he may have let the sliding door to the patio open and maybe Ghost got out. Pop quickly added that he didn't think that scenario was very likely because it's hard to miss a large white dog, even at night.

David said maybe they should drive around the neighborhood and look for Ghost.

Kathy quickly scotched that idea. Her problems had started with driving around in the dark at night, and she thought she'd just rather go to bed and deal with the dog issue in the morning.

Pop felt like he had escaped a bullet.

As it turned out, there was still another round or two in the chamber.

First, Pop slept in late, failing to get up and look for Ghost at the lake like he had planned. Then David pounded on his door and gave him hell when he opened it. Your behavior is just … irresponsible, David sputtered. I mean, hell, we entrusted you to look out after our dog. David demanded to come in and see if Pop was keeping the dog in the apartment. After David convinced himself that he wasn't, he lobbed another bomb, accusing Pop of stealing the dog so he could sell it and make a profit. For Jews it always comes down to money, Pop thought. Really, Pop said, that was the last thing on my mind when I offered to watch your stupid dog. As a parting shot, Pop told him that the dog probably ran away because David and Kathy were mean to it.

Pop was pretty upset after his conversation with David, and he decided he better put things on the record, just in case the situation got worse. He went to the Palm Glades Police Department and filed a report of a missing dog. (You might think the owners would have thought of that, he huffed.) Pop told the officer who took the report that he didn't want this to come back on him, that why he was reporting it, and that's why he wanted the incident to be on file. The officer who took the report just shrugged. We have enough trouble finding missing people, he said. Don't get your hopes up that we'll find the missing dog.

As soon as he got back home, Kathy came by and told Pop he would have to move. Now? he asked. Now, she told him. I mean you can have a few days to find another place to stay, but you have to get out of here. I mean it, buddy. I really do.

Pop lamented his situation to Dale across the street, who agreed that it was a tough situation and the penalty was pretty harsh. Why don't you get your stuff, Dale said, and move in with me? Pop took him up on it. He didn't have many possessions – hell, he could fit most of his stuff in a navel orange crate – and the move didn't take any time at all. David watched him as he packed his things, making sure, Pop figured, that Pop wasn't going to steal anything.

Pop stayed with Dale throughout most of 2005 and well into 2006. He didn't see much of David and Kathy after that, and he never learned whether they got their dog back. Over time, he didn't see the Lexus in the driveway quite as often, and after a while, it hardly appeared at all. Every once in a while, he would see Kathy in the yard, and she still looked good to him, as sexy and as fuckable as he remembered. But Pop was damaged goods to her, and he knew it was pointless to try to come on to her, after all the water that had come between them.

Pop and Dale, who was an NOC technician, worked different shifts, so they were mostly like two ships passing in the night all the time. Plus, Dale was out a lot when he wasn't working: he spent most of his time at the telecommunications center where he worked facing a video wall so he wasn't into watching TV when he got home. Consequently, he ate out a lot and went to the range a lot, occasionally taking Pop with him, if Pop was free. He was also into golf (yuck!) and hiking, which Pop wasn't, and took vacations in places like the Smokey Mountains so he could tromp around in the woods and get lost.

In May, Dale helped Pop celebrate his 21st birthday by taking him to a gun store, where Pop bought himself a so-called "Wonder Nine" – a 9 mm Glock 19 semiautomatic handgun. Pop had thought about getting a Smith & Wesson M-669, but decided against it because of S&W's collusion with the Clinton administration, which had mandated a 10 round mag instead of the standard 15 rounds and got S&W to come out with a version of its x9 series that was equipped with the government mandated mag. (It was Dale who set him straight on this.) In any event, Pop was happy with the Glock. It wasn't as neat-looking as the Smith & Wesson, but it was readily concealable and had the 15 rounds. Pop spent a lot of time that summer shooting with the Glock, and he got pretty good at it, if he might say. He could shoot within just under three inches with it from a distance of 25 yards.

In late August just before Labor Day, Pop got a call

from his friend, Kenny G. KG told him that mum had cornered Keilah in a local Giant Eagle, pulling her hair and calling her a whore, and got arrested for disorderly conduct.

Oh, shit, Pop said.

That's not why I'm calling, KG told him. Seems that your mum found your shotgun, and … and … and . … KG gulped hard over the phone.

And what? Pop asked.

She tried to kill herself, KG said.

Pop pictured a ghastly scene with blood all over the walls and pieces of Evelyn's skull and brain blown all over their house. Is she dead? he asked Kenny G.

No, KG told him. She missed herself completely. But she blew the hell out of the ceiling fan in your dining room, the one you and I installed, remember?

Yeah, I remember. Evelyn's okay?

She's in Western Psych. And your gran is in a county home. Might be a good time for you to come home and help put the pieces back together. Your decision, of course, KG said, I'm just saying.

Pop said he would be leaving in the morning. Then he told Dale, and loaded his shit in his truck. Before he left, there was one thing he had to do.

Pop drove up to Lake Peel. He drove through the boating area, past all the alligator warning signs, and pulled right up to the beach. It was already dusk, and you could barely see anything. Pop took his shirt off and his pants, stripping down to his underwear. Then he jumped in and started swimming. He swam out into the lake as far as he could, dog paddling for a little bit when he started feeling tired. He looked back at the beach, and there was a purple hue where the sky met the shore. Pop thought he could see the lights from Palm Glades in the distance, but it may have just been the haze rising from the swampy lake. Pop splashed around in the water, telling anything that might be out there with him, or gliding past him in the dark, that he was around. Once, as he drifted further out on the lake, he thought he saw something that looked like a log float past, and a patch of something yellow in the moon glow; later, he felt something nudge his toes, but whatever it was it didn't come any closer. Pop stayed out in the lake for what seemed like forever, the water up to his chin and his fingers and toes getting all wrinkly, the way they do when you have been in the bath too long. When he came in, he put his shirt and pants back on, and drove back to Palm Glades. After he had showered and dried himself off, he thanked Dale for being a good friend. They had a couple of beers together, but neither of them talked much. Finally, Dale remarked that he had a job to do and it was time to say goodbye. Pop stayed up for a while looking at the stars in the Florida sky.

The next morning, he drove the one thousand one hundred and twenty-one miles from Palm Glades to Pittsburgh. It took him close to 17 hours to do it. He stopped a couple of times for gas, but he never looked back, not once along the way.

Homeboy

From one man's perspective, Pop didn't know how good he had it. If he wanted to get on a bus and go to Florida, he could do it. If he wanted to jump inside his new used Ford F-150 and go to a convenience store for a fresh pack of cigarettes, there wasn't anything stopping him. Hell, if he just wanted to get up off the couch and stroll down the hall to the bathroom, no problem. There wasn't anything holding him back. He didn't have to ask anyone for permission.

Death row isn't like that at all. You are not free to move about the country. You are not free to go anywhere at all. Your freedom has been forfeited, and your rights – to walk outside, to breathe fresh air, to feel the sun on your face, to run in the rain with your tongue outstretched to catch the raindrops as they fall – have been extinguished.

I've tried to tell you what solitary confinement is like, what it feels like to be locked in a cell with a footprint no bigger than a throw rug for up to 23 hours a day. Hell, even Stephen Hawking gets to leave his room every now and then; in fact, he once left the planet, taking a zero gravity air flight in 2007. He may be imprisoned in his body, but he's not imprisoned in a space.

What I haven't talked about is the system of control that keeps me locked up here. I haven't talked about what I have to go through to leave this cell for the one or two hours a day that I can go to the prison library, or the cage that passes for an exercise room. Except for one brief riff on body cavity searches, I haven't talked about the bullshit I have to wade through to see my lawyer or just to take a shower.

I haven't talked about the guards, aka the correctional officers, as they like to be called in our hip new age of politically correct terminology where "guard" is considered demeaning. (If you ask me, the word "prisoner," like the word, "convict," or "con," is demeaning, too. Of course, unlike COs, prisoners don't have professional training, or at least they don't get it until they become part of the general prison population and get some lessons from those who know how crime should be done. Perhaps they should call it a schoolhouse instead of a prison, or, I'm sorry, a correctional facility.)

Death row Pennsylvania is a hall of fame for prison guards, I mean, COs. The most notorious one was Charles Graner, who practiced his craft here stateside before going on to perfect it overseas at Abu Ghraib.

At SCI-Fayette, his first stop in the Pennsylvania corrections system, Graner was accused of putting mace in a new CO's coffee cup, causing the man to get sick.

At SCI-Greene, a prisoner accused him of putting a razor blade in his food, and punching and kicking him when Graner took him to the nurse after the prisoner had bit into it.

He was sued once for tripping a prisoner after handcuffing him and making him stand on one foot, but the suit was later thrown out because the statute of limitations had expired.

At Abu Ghraib, Graner threw food into toilets and ordered prisoners to fetch it out and eat it.

He punched one prisoner in the head so hard the man lost consciousness.

He sodomized another with a phosphoric light.

And, of course, he supervised all those photographs, the ones that showed his girlfriend holding a naked Iraqi on a leash and himself giving a thumbs-up sign over naked inmates piled into a pyramid, not to mention the iconic one of a man standing on a box with electrical wires attached to his hands and penis.

Graner once explained himself by saying that "The Christian in me says, 'it's wrong,' but the corrections officer in me says, 'I love to make a grown man piss himself.'"

(Graner, by the way, grew up in Pittsburgh, like Pop. Maybe there's something in the cultural waters.)

Graner was gone before I got here, having been sent off to serve time in a federal prison in Kansas for what he did at Abu Ghraib.

And no, I can't say that I've been put on a box and wired to electrodes, or made to wear a leash, or any of those other weird things that were done to Iraqi prisoners at Abu Ghraib.

But I have been cuffed in the head by prison guards, had my food thrown on the floor, and even been made to piss myself on occasion.

Of course, there's the daily humiliation that occurs every time I get to leave my cell, when I am ordered to stand on a blanket, face the wall, remove my prison jumpsuit, underwear and socks, and expose myself to four prison guards. Two of them stand ready with raised batons while a third puts on a pair of rubber gloves and a fourth barks commands:

"Lift your arms.

Bend over.

Spread your cheeks."

This is the quality of my everyday interactions with my captors. Believe me, there is nothing about being strip-searched by some dude with a gun on his hip that fosters any kind of intimacy. But it's not just having to stand naked in front of some guy you don't know while he orders you at gunpoint to bend over, it's knowing that your captor regards you as something less than a human being, as some subspecies of human that's more like a grunting animal than a man. I am the monster under the bed, the boogeyman, the creature from the deep. I can see it in the eyes of the COs. They look at me warily, untrustingly, suspiciously, the way one looks at a coiled snake. I am the devil creature who crapped in the garden and got everyone else thrown out, Adam, Eve, the whole fucking caboodle. My crime, in their eyes, justifies the most horrible kind of treatment, far worse than they think I get – and believe me they would make it worse for me if they thought they could get away with it. Oftentimes, they can.

I've gotten used to being treated like an animal, some subspecies of man (and by the way, I don't blame the COs for this – they're just reflecting public sentiment), but I haven't reconciled my mind to the feeling I get every time I get a little taste of inmate freedom -- a shower, a workout, a visit – and return to my cell to find that it has been invaded, that someone has gone through my things and rearranged them or even taken something that he considers to be contraband, forbidden, like the paper cup I saved from my dinner tray or a letter from my lawyer. The message is that my things do not really belong to me, that there is nothing to which I truly can claim ownership, that there is just some stuff that has been loaned to me but can never be mine in principle and that can be taken away from me at any moment, on the slightest provocation, or for no reason at all.

I am convinced, for example, that someone has been looking at this manuscript (sometimes, the pages are out of sequence and I don't remember reshuffling them), reading it while I am gone, and laughing about it to the other COs behind my back. I am afraid, it is my darkest fear, really, that I will leave here one day to exercise or to shower and return to find that my writing is gone. I really don't know what I would do if that were to happen.

***

Well, it was true: Mum was so incompetent she couldn't even kill herself. When Pop got home, he inspected the dining room and saw the damage the Maverick had done to the ceiling fan, the ceiling and the wall. The shotgun blast had blown the fan out of its fixture and the spreading pellets had pockmarked the ceiling so bad it looked like Manuel Noreiga's face. The wall wasn't any better; apparently, Mum wasn't satisfied with the damage she had done to the ceiling so she took aim a second time at one of the walls, making a holey mess and, in the process, shattering the frame on a picture of Sugar Pop and Gran when they were young. They would never look that young again, Pop thought as he picked up the shattered glass. He also concluded that it would take forever to dig the buckshot out of the ceiling and the walls, and figured it might be better just to plaster over it.

Mum didn't look a whole hell of a lot better than the ceiling. She was shaking like the proverbial leaf when he went to get her out of Western Psych and she wobbled like jelly as he escorted her from the place. She had lost a lot of weight and her hair was frightful and she went on and on in a monotone voice about the nightmares that she was having, several of which involved a Medusa-like Keilah, snakes coiling around her face, and one in which Pop got eaten by an alligator. (For real? he asked her. No, shitting you, she said.) She also kept getting these flashes of light in her eyeballs, even when her eyes were closed, and she felt like maggots were crawling all over her skin, trying to get inside her, to eat her from within. The doctor who treated her gave Pop a prescription for some benzodiazepines to help get mum through the withdrawal process.

When he got her home, she told him about the altercation with Keilah. According to mum, she had rounded an aisle in the local Giant Eagle and there was Keilah, blocking her path with a shopping cart. You know, I was just innocently minding my own business, Evelyn said, but that slut whore ex-girlfriend of yours wouldn't let me past. So I spat in her face, and took up a fighting stance, and said, okay, come on and bring it. I mean, like what did she expect?

KG told him there was more to it than that and he believed mum had been stalking Keilah for months. She showed up a couple of times at the Eat'n Park at the Waterworks, but Keilah wasn't there, and the management pretty much thought she was harmless, even though she would tank up on Smiley cookies and iced tea and talk in a tiny baby voice. She blamed Keilah for driving you away from her. She really loves you, KG said.

Mum loves me? Pop asked.

Loves and missed you while you were gone, KG answered.

Did she say that?

Not in those exact words, KG told him.

Pop nonetheless decided that he would look after mum and nurse her back to health. Thus began the game they would play with each other over the next couple of months. It was called Hide the Bottle. Mum would hide a bottle of booze somewhere and Pop would find it and stash it away somewhere else where mum couldn't get her hands on it and go on another bender. The task was made easier for Pop by the fact that mum would always buy BIG cheap bottles of alcohol – gut rot gin rockin', 151 proof rum in the 1.75 ml. size, that kind of stuff. She would have even bought Everclear 191 proof natural grain alcohol if you didn't need a license to buy it in Pennsylvania. Pop confided to KG that it was a good thing mum didn't have a preference for those tiny airline size bottles, or he would never had been able to catch her.

Their daily routine was to watch TV. They watched Live with Regis and Kelly in the morning (mum loved Regis), followed by Judge Alex, which involved such burning issues of the day as deciding whether or not to believe the landlord who said her rental house was in great shape until this couple moved in and clogged the pipes with paper towels and hair weaves. Mum sided with the landlord, but Pop, knowing how landlords tend to blame their tenants (hell, he knew of one who said her tenant had lost her dog), saw the case somewhat differently. Does there always have to be someone to blame? he asked Evelyn, but, of course, she said yes.

At noon, they watched local news. Mum liked KDKA because it didn't just repeat its 11 o'clock news like WPXI did, and she was partial to Stacey Smith, but Pop hated Patrice King Brown, his co-host (and not just because she was black.) Consequently, most days, Pop would get up and search the web and get the real news, the news you couldn't find on TV, from Stormtroop or Alex Jones or even Glenn Beck ("The Fusion of Entertainment and Enlightenment"), who had free streaming audio of his program 24/7.

In the afternoon, they watched Judge Joe Brown (whom Pop also hated), Jerry Springer (of course), Steve Wilcos (who would make his guests take lie-detector tests and ask them questions about their affairs in front of their wives and girlfriends, and other crap like that), and the Channel 4 Action News at 5.

While they were watching TV, Pop had Evelyn make up a list of the things that would make her want to drink – situations, events, or people, certain songs, or even smells – so-called "relapse triggers" as the alcoholic relapse prevention people like to call them. Evelyn catalogued every holiday, every shift in season, every weekend, every Monday, Tuesday, Wednesday, Thursday and Friday. Her people names included everyone she knew, and there wasn't a song ever sung that Evelyn couldn't relate to drinking. Even such a banal thing as walking down the aisle in a grocery store could get her mind to drinking – the grapes in the fruit aisle would remind her of wine, the barley in the baking aisle of beer, and the Nutra-Grain in the cereal aisle made her think of vodka. Then, of course, there was the Nyquil and the rubbing alcohol near the pharmacy.

Pop sometimes tried to encourage her to go outside for a walk – but sunshine made her thirst for a cold one on the veranda. Blustery days, in contrast, were just perfect for a hot toddy. Pop concluded that it was better for Evelyn to remain inside, but he inwardly suspected that being alone in a room with her son and a TV set was the biggest trigger of all.

Sometimes, in the course of a long TV-watching day, Pop would fall asleep in the easy chair, and wake up to find mum gone. (This was when she bought those BIG bottles of the cheap booze she drank.) Once he determined she was out, Pop typically swung into action, putting his own patented Alcoholic Relapse Prevention Plan in motion, which usually just involved walking up to the Lyceum and finding mum at the bar, or waiting outside the state store until she came out with her purchases.

Of course, there were other times when Pop just said, Aw, screw it, and used the time to fantasize about one of the chicks he saw on TV or to dig into his memory bank for images of Keilah or Kathy, and jacked himself off (imaging Keilah or Kelly [Kathy?] was risky, however, as the memories they engendered were as likely to be a total sexual buzz kill as to give him a boner).

(Although he didn't know it at the time, his sexual

fantasy life was ideal preparation for prison, and conditioned him for the years that lay ahead.)

Pop didn't know if mum was worse when she was sober or worse when she was drunk. When she was sober, she affected a little girl's voice, high-pitched and whiny, that drove Pop out of his mind. When she was drunk, her voice was lower-pitched, but her language was very coarse and her tone unremittingly abusive, sort of the Second Coming of Sugar-Pop in the vulgarity department, but without any of his grandfather's redeeming jocularity. If she was sober and wanted a drink, mum would go on about what a good son Pop was and how very much she loved him, the transparency of her affection for him revealing just how desperately she wanted a drink. If she was drunk and Pop wanted her to stop, she would tell him over and over again what a lousy good-for-nothing bastard he was, emphasizing the bastard part way too much, as if she couldn't refrain from reminding him that she was unmarried when he was born.

The soprano Evelyn he hated and the alto Evelyn he despised. The problem was he simply couldn't stand his mother's voice. But if he tried to escape her, to put himself out of earshot, so to speak, he felt like he was contributing to her relapse. And, of course, if he didn't, if he stayed to face the unmusic, as it were, he found himself wishing for her to relapse.

Ultimately, it wasn't his call, of course. Evelyn was going to do whatever Evelyn wanted. And it was perfectly clear to Pop that the one thing Evelyn wanted to do more than anything else in the world was to drink herself to death.

He shifted tactics. If he couldn't prevent her from

drinking, he could try to keep her from hurting herself or anyone else with the bad luck to cross her path. He wasn't sure you could really prevent someone from committing suicide, but he decided he would try.

(Billy Till might still be around, if Pop had been in charge of SCI-Garrow.)

He bought a gun safe for the Maverick. (The police had taken it after Evelyn's suicide attempt, but Pop asked for it back as soon as he got home. For safety's sake, he had buried it in the yard, a temporary measure to be sure, out of fear mum might get her hands on it. He thought of burying it in the park again, but the whole Keilah business dissuaded him from this idea.) The safe was a V-Line Closet model, which he installed in his room. It was big enough to hold a couple of rifles and/or shotguns, plus it had a pegboard door panel with plenty of places to hang a pistol rack or two and had enough shelf space inside to store his ammunition. It also had a mechanical push button lock with a programmable combination. Pop decided to keep the combination partially complete, so he could get to the Maverick as quickly as possible if he needed it. The safe set him back $569.50. Pop had thought about getting a Mossberg clamp or Loc-Box, which would have been a whole hell of a lot cheaper, but he figured it would only be a stopgap solution anyway and wouldn't accommodate the Bersa or any other guns he might want to buy.

Pop also took their cutlery and stashed it at KG's house, replacing their knives, forks and spoons with plastic. He made an inventory of other sharp objects in the house, such as Evelyn's garden shears, and spirited them off to KG's, too.

One day, after he had safety-proofed the house as much as he could, he drove up to the Kane Hospital in Glen-Hazel to see how Gran was doing. The home was a big red brick building located up the hill from the Eat'n Park where Keilah used to work. It saddened Pop to go there. What he saw when he got inside saddened him even more. Gran was all shriveled and pale and boney, a shock of white hair atop a frame so thin it could almost be mistaken for a broom handle. (She reminded him of a puppet he had seen in a special collection of the Heinz History Center that had a mop of rug yarn hair and a large wooden nose). Gran's mouth drooped to one side, and her right shoulder looked as if it had separated from the socket – it hung idly at her side. Pop figured Gran had had another stroke.

He leaned over her and took one of her boney aged hands in his and told her, "Hey Gran, it's Pop."

She looked up at him in wide-eyed amazement. "Who are you?" she asked, slobbering, her mouth struggling to form words.

"Pop, Little Pop, don't you remember me?"

Gran pulled her hand away from him, and turned her mop yarn head on the pillow.

"Paw –aw - op," he said, elongating the word, as if he were talking to a child.

She brought her head back and brought him back into focus.

"Home," she said. "Home, home, home, home, home."

Pop was perplexed. He didn't know what Gran was trying to tell him.

"Home, home, home," she insisted repeatedly.

"You want me to take you home? Is that what you're trying to tell me?"

Gran opened her eyes wide and gurgled back at him. "Home, home, home," she said.

"Well, Gran, " Pop said, "I don't think I could do that. I think your nurses and doctors think you belong here."

"HOME!" Gran insisted.

"Plus," Pop said, "it wouldn't be the best place for you at all." Especially not with Evelyn falling back off the wagon, Pop said to himself.

"I know who you are," Gran said suddenly.

"Pop," Pop said, tapping himself on the chest. "Pop. It's me."

"You're not Pop," Gran said.

"Sure it's me. Pop," he repeated to her. "Pa – aw – op."

"Not Pop," Gran insisted.

"No? Well who am I then," Pop said with a rising tone of indignation.

Gran tapped him in the breastbone with a boney finger. "You're a coward," she said.

"Gran!" Pop replied in protest, but his grandmother was reforming the syllables of the name she had just called him, mouthing the word coward but without any sound coming out at all. Spittle dribbled down her chin in spurts as she worked her jaw. Her unruly grey hair stuck out from her head like twine, making her look like a Fury. Coward, she lisped. When she was finished spitting out the word, Gran turned her aged face toward the wall, and Pop knew his visit with her was over.

***

When he got back home, Pop found Evelyn entwined on the couch with some guy. Hi, my name is Lou, he announced, as he pawed mother's breasts. Pop thought about pulling him off of Evelyn and dragging him into the bedroom where his gun cabinet was and forcing the barrel of the Maverick down his throat. But Lou was just another in a long line of Evelyn's alkie fuck buddies and Pop figured he wasn't worth the trouble.

Pop went into his room and closed the door. Before he emerged, he had written a resume, one he hand-delivered or mailed to practically every window-fitting company in western Pennsylvania. His effort did not succeed in landing him a job. Pop went to an employment agency, but the only openings were for people who were already employed. Pop tried Manpower and some of the other temporary help places, but they didn't have anything for someone without a high school diploma. What's more, Pop was ineligible for unemployment compensation because he had voluntarily left his last job. Welfare gave him food stamps and some minimal cash assistance, which wasn't enough to keep him in cigarettes.

THE POLITICIZATION OF PETER POPOVICH, PART 3

Glenn Beck told him that illegal immigrants were taking American jobs, the ones that weren't already outsourced to India, or wherever. Why even some liberals agreed that immigrants take jobs that were once held by, or would otherwise go to, American-born workers like Pop. Because Pittsburgh wasn't New York, Pop couldn't say he saw Pakistanis driving taxicabs everywhere, Mexicans waiting tables, or Salvadorans doing construction work, but, it seemed that every other health care worker was from a foreign country and the Asians had definitely taken over the city's high tech jobs. My people were here first, he wanted to tell them. Those jobs are ours!

Sugar-Pop's father, Pavel, had come to America from Serbia when he was 18. He hailed from the Vranje region of the country and spelled his last name Popovic´ with the accent mark over the c; the surname meant "family or son of a priest." Pavel married Pop's great grandmother, Kaazimiri Kovac, who was Croatian, and whose parents brought her to this country when she was only 12. By Pop's rough estimation, the Popoviches had been in the United States for nigh on one hundred years. That tenure should count for something, Pop believed.

Blue collar people like the Popoviches didn't institute slavery (they weren't here then) but they got blamed for being racists when they squawked about losing jobs to affirmative action applicants or objected to their schools becoming experimental laboratories for forced busing. Meanwhile, the Mayflower people, the DAR'ers, and all the other blue bloods were benefiting from nepotism in the office and legacy preferences in college admissions and just about everywhere else. They didn't have to worry about desegregation busing because the United States Supreme Court had drawn a line in Milliken v. Bradley, exempting white suburban schools from the mandates that applied to inner-city schools.

Now the Popoviches (those of them that hadn't fled to the suburbs after Bradley), were on the front lines again. This time, the battle was between the native born and the foreign, and the Popoviches were getting shit for complaining that illegal immigrants were taking their jobs, spiking crime and overburdening their schools and putting a strain on their communities, and siphoning off tax dollars in the process. It was okay when the Mayflowers looked down on the sheeny Irish or crapped all over the Italians and the Serbians and the Poles. But to object that NAFTA wasn't good for white middle-class Americans was somehow a badge of prejudice – notwithstanding evidence that NAFTA was a body blow to the real wages of American workers (and impoverished Mexican farmers, too.)

It made Pop mad. Every time he got a letter in the mail telling him a job he had applied for had gone to someone else, he felt like globalization was a plot to get him personally, and that people like Bill Clinton, who signed NAFTA into law, were trying to stick their Yale law degrees, Rhodes scholarships and liberal pedigrees up his butt. In the New World Order, that Clinton and all the other liberals were creating (with plenty of help from so-called conservatives like George Herbert Walker Bush, who dreamed up NAFTA in the first place), there wouldn't be room for people like Peter Popovich. There would be the master class and the servants. The servants would be subject to a uniform system of laws administered by world courts that would essentially determine who lived where, who got what, who could have children, who would get fed, even who lived or died. Private property would be abolished and privately owned firearms would be outlawed. The master class, of course, would suffer no privations under the New World Order, because their wealth and privilege would exempt them from obedience to the laws. Consequently, they could have their McMansions, their six thousand dollar shower curtains, their acres of diamonds, and to hell with everyone else.

It was wrong, the New World Order. It was evil. Someday, somehow, someone would have to rise up against it and try to bring it down. Pop wanted to be there when it happened. He wanted to be on the front lines of that war.

Nix N

Menace has a name. Out of discretion and other more self-interested reasons that should shortly become clear, I won't mention the name here, but it belongs to a certain CO. A few days ago, I was being strip-searched in my cell prior to being taken to the exercise pen when a CO leaned over and whispered in my ear, "You're writing a book, so what? You know you're still a criminal." I felt like he had punched me. I wanted to do something, strike back in some fashion, but there were too many CO's in my cell to allow me to respond physically and my usual knack for words failed me at the time. I fully expected that this manuscript would be gone when I returned to my cell after my exercise period was over. It wasn't, but someone had clearly gone through my things. My glasses weren't where I left them, and I even suspected that someone had been trying them on. The glasses are special order ones with prescription lenses that are thicker and heavier than ordinary lenses – they use "lighthouse" lenses or prismlets and are prescribed to correct my occasional double vision. In any event, something didn't feel right when I put them on; they didn't set quite right on the bridge of my nose and didn't fit as snugly against my temples. I also noticed that one of my shower sandals was gone, which really honked me off. I feared that my manuscript might be confiscated or stolen, too, and I wondered what I could do to prevent that from happening.

I bitched about the shower sandal to the CO who brought me dinner and, later, I asked the observation officer for permission to go to the Law Library, and used my subsequently scheduled time there to research my legal rights. I learned that there had once been laws in place that prevented prisoners from writing. These legal barriers were struck down with the help of a California Death Row inmate named Caryl Chessman, who encoded his literary work in putative "legal documents" and smuggled them out of jail. He mailed one of his manuscripts to his lawyer and it became the subject of a court case after the warden demanded the manuscript back (on the grounds that it was the product of prison labor) and sued Chessman's lawyer and publisher when they refused to return it. The landmark case was Davis v. Superior Court, 175 Cal. App. 2d 8 (1959). Excuse me for sounding like a jailhouse lawyer now, but it held that the warden couldn't prevent Chessman from writing. The court was especially incensed with the warden's argument that the state "owned" Chessman's manuscript. It said, "[a]n odor of totalitarianism infects the concept that any product of the prisoner's mind automatically becomes the property of the state. While a free society recognizes the social need for incarceration of offenders, it claims no possession of their minds."

Yeah, I know, you couldn't give a rat's ass for prisoners' minds, but the Davis case told me I had some arrows in my quiver if SCI-Garrow tried to take my manuscript. My big fear, of course, was that a certain CO would simply destroy it. So I took a page from Chessman's book, and decided to mail what I have written so far to my lawyer. I have the right under prison rules and regulations to mail whatever I want to my lawyer without fear of censorship (not that I believe that). I figure that if my book gets burnt or shredded or simply lost because someone here doesn't like the fact I'm writing, I can talk to Ronni Silverstein about it the next time I see her, and she can file a Civil Complaint on my behalf (or maybe I'll just go on a goddamn hunger strike.) That's where I am right now. The drawback is that I can't go back and read what I've already written (they don't allow Death Row inmates to keep copies of letters and other written materials here), and my book may suffer from continuity problems or whatever as a result (I often repeat repeat myself, I often repeat repeat). But that's a risk I'm willing to take.

I've pledged myself that each time I finish a chapter, I'll mail it to Silverstein. I guess that when I started this book, I thought I would send it out of here when I was finished, and it would kind of be like setting foot outside this prison, a way of securing a little bit of metaphorical freedom for myself in the end. Now, it's like sending myself out in pieces – a leg here, an arm, a hand – and knowing that when I finally release the last part of me, I'll be gone. I never liked that stupid song by Cat Stevens or Yusuf Islam or whatever the hell he's calling himself now, but now at least I feel that I understand it. When I mail out the last chapter of this book, I won't have to talk (no more.)

Chessman, by the way, was executed for forcing a 17-year old girl to perform oral sex (and people thought impeachment was harsh). The execution was put off eight times. The ninth time it was scheduled, a judge's secretary called the warden to tell him a stay had been granted. She dialed the wrong number first, and, by the time she got connected to the warden, Chessman had been strapped in the gas chamber, and the execution had already begun. The warden didn't want to stop it and open the chamber doors for fear of gassing one or more of the 60 spectators who were there to witness Chessman's death. (One of them was a red-haired reporter named Eleanor Gardner Black; Chessman smiled at her through the glass). So the onlookers got what they came for and Chessman went to his death, even though a reprieve had been granted. Some cats really do have nine lives, I guess, and Chessman had used up all of his.

***

The phone call took Pop completely by surprise. He had applied for a job with Brackenridge Window more than six months before he got the phone call, and when he hadn't received an instantaneous reply, he assumed he would never hear from them at all. They guy on the phone said they had a guy quit on them and were looking for someone with window fitting experience who could start immediately to replace him. I'm your guy, Pop said.

They were true to their word and put him to work on a renovation project right away. The project was in Butler and involved converting an old hospital into condominiums. There were hundreds of windows in the building that had to be removed and replaced.

Jack, his foreman, recommended that Pop get a room

in Butler so he wouldn't have to drive the 80 miles or so back and forth from Pittsburgh every day. Pop thought that was a good idea. He needed some space between himself and Evelyn and Lou. But Pop couldn't find an apartment that suited him, and the cheapest motel room he could find cost more than $30 a day. Pop was making less than $20 an hour for a 30 to 40 hour week, and the math just didn't work. He decided he would have to commute.

This turned out to be a mistake. The traffic on Routes 28 and 8 was worse than he had expected, even going against the flow, and Jack expected him to be on site by daybreak. Pop was late one time his first week on the job and a couple of times during the second, and Jack told him that if he were late again he'd can him.

What's more, the guys on Pop's crew didn't like him. There was some old guy named Sweeney who kept asking him who taught him how to measure. Some of the windows on the project had to be cut and framed, rather than just replaced, a task that required a router, which Pop had never used before. He had done some framing and cutting in Florida with a circ saw, and when he mentioned that to Sweeney, the dude went ballistic. Are you nuts? he said. A router's faster and cleaner than a circ saw. Didn't they teach you nothin' down in Florida?

One morning, Jack bitched him out when he found him up on a ladder. The ladder didn't extend high enough, so Pop had propped it up on some scaffolding he found lying around on site. Jack screamed at him to tie it off. Do that again, make sure you tie off the ladder at the top, Jack said when Pop was back on the ground. OSHA gets on my ass because you don't know how to set up a ladder, so I'm going to get on yours. Plus you fall off of there and hurt yourself, man, you're on your own. You signed an independent contractor agreement with this company and it doesn't require us to pay your medical bills or any workers compensation if you get hurt.

Pop moped around a bit after Jack screamed at him, but Sweeney said Jack was just looking after him, and that was more than he would do, dumb ass. (Sweeney also told him that a former member of their crew had failed to tie off his ladder and fell, shattering the bones in his feet, arms, chest and back. Jack felt really bad about it, and it was hard on the rest of them, too, requiring them to work a man short, which was why they were all expecting Pop to do more than show up, if he could manage that trick in the first place.)

Then there was Nixon. (Pop called him "Nix N," which, as you can figure out, was a private slur that substituted for a racial epithet.) He had the same last name as one of Pop's heroes, and, as luck would have it, he had the same first name, too. Ordinarily, this would have engendered some sympathy in Pop, and not just because of the political and iconic significance of Richard Nixon's name. You would think two guys whose first names – Peter and Dick – had so much in common wouldn't have any trouble getting along with each other. You'd be wrong. Dick Nixon, who didn't resemble President Nixon in the slightest, was a big, fat black guy who liked to torment Pop at least once a week by asking him if he was getting any pussy. The first time Nixon asked, Pop didn't quite know how to answer it (hell, it was none of Nixon's business really) so he simply ignored him, which played right into Nixon's game. "You ain't getting any," Nixon declared. The he went around to everyone on the worksite and told them "Pop ain't getting no pussy. He probably ain't ever even seen a pussy – other than his own."

His day devolved into a bitter routine of getting up at o' dark thirty, getting showered and dressed and slipping out sometimes just as Evelyn and Lou were coming home from the bar, where they often stayed long after last call. Then it was off to Butler, negotiating the early morning traffic on Route 28, and stopping off at a McDonalds near the work site so he could buy coffee for everyone on the crew (as the youngest one of them, the one with the least seniority, that was his designated task). Pop would keep a little slip of paper in his pocket where he had written down everyone's order – coffee, double sugar, double cream; coffee double cream, no sugar; coffee, no cream, two sweet 'n low; coffee black, and so forth. If he forgot the slip, or the McDonalds girl messed up the order, there would be hell to pay when he arrived at the work site. There was all this bullshit to go through, just so he could be at work by 6 o'clock and some summer mornings even earlier.

Of course, once he got to work, Nixon would be waiting for him with the inevitable query, "Get any pussy last night?" And people wondered why Pop had an attitude about niggers.

He tried to keep his politics under wraps and not on his sleeve like some people. Nixon, for example, was always mouthing off about President Bush. Bush was a liar. That was Nixon's mantra. He lied to the country about WMD's. He lied to get the nation into Iraq. He even lied about his service record and being AWOL while he was supposed to be at an Air National Guard unit in Montgomery, Alabama. He lied about his two DWI's and his cocaine use. He lied about his ties to Enron and Ken Lay. He lied about his cozy relationship with the Saudis, whom he held hands with and was secretly in bed with. He lied about this. And he lied about that. Lie lie lie lie lie lie. And when he wasn't lying he was just being wrong and stupid. A veritable Alfred E. Newman.

Well, if Bill Clinton had been so smart, he'd have kept his cock out of some young girl's mouth, and he would still be president, Pop said one day in a moment of pure exasperation.

To his surprise, Sweeney and Edzel, another guy on their crew, took Nixon's side and laughed at Pop.

Pop doesn't know the president is limited to two terms, Edzel said. Pop can't count to eight, Sweeney said, adding that it didn't surprise him because he had seen Pop measure.

You know what I meant, Pop grumbled.

But they didn't.

Pop tried to engage Nixon once on the Iraqi war, but Nixon, who proclaimed that the war was a BIG BIG MISTAKE, wasn't interested in even so much as listening to another point of view. Pop tried to tell him that Saddam Hussein was a tyrant who modeled himself after Joseph Stalin. Why, he had a library full of books about Stalin and boasted that he would turn Iraq into a Stalinist state. He came close. He murdered as many as a million people. He created a torture state, instilling fear in everyone under his regime. He may not have had WMD's, but he secretly funded the Pakistani A-bomb program and A. Q. Khan, the Pakistani scientist in charge of that program, once offered to build him an A-bomb in return. He used chemical weapons in the Iran-Iraq war. He gassed the Kurds. He was the world's greatest serial killer at the time we declared war on him. (This guy Christopher Hitchens, who used to be a liberal, said in a magazine piece that Saddam was the reincarnation of Jeffrey Dahmer. – Saddahmer Hussein, he called him.) It was right to take him out.

Nixon just looked at him and said, "So, you still ain't getting' any pussy, are you?"

Pop suspected that Sweeney and Edzel, and most of the other guys on the crew, shared his political opinions and views and just didn't want to express them in front of Nixon. But he didn't really know because he didn't socialize with his co-workers after the work day was done. They would go off to drink at their favorite local watering hole, but Pop never got invited.

It was probably a good thing he didn't get to exchange views with Sweeney and Edzel. Who knows how much that may have upped the ante in the tension game that was Pop's job. Hell, they were probably fucking Democrats. Pop's own political views were in a state of flux anyway. Although he liked George Bush, he knew the president's father was one of the architects of the "New World Order" – Papa Bush had invoked the phrase in a speech he made after Desert Storm -- and Pop figured George II was probably part of the conspiracy, too.

He became sure of it sometime after May 4, 2007, when the White House posted on its web page part of a directive called National Security and Homeland Security Presidential Directive NSPD-51. It was accompanied by another directive call NSPD-20. Together, they gave the

Executive sweeping powers to annex the congressional and judicial branches of government and roll them all up into one in the event of "a catastrophic emergency."

THE POLITICIZATION OF PETER POPOVICH, PART 4

Jerome Corsi, the guy who spearheaded the drive to swift boat John Kerry, publically exposing Kerry as a liar when he claimed to have fought in Cambodia, when he was nowhere near the fucking place (and if he lied about that, who knew what other lies he told or was willing to tell), said that the directive gave the president the power to seize property and take over privately held companies, to institute martial law, to take over transportation and public communication, to restrict travel and, in a variety of other ways, control the citizens of the United States.

The directive defined catastrophe as "any incident, regardless of location, that results in extraordinary levels of mass casualties, damage or disruption severely affecting the U.S. population, infrastructure, environment, economy or government function."

Hell, Pop figured, that could apply to the Oklahoma bombings or the siege of Waco or any other perceived threat. Hell, it could apply to just about anything.

Pop read that the new directive was built on an old one called Readiness Exercise 1984, or Rex 84, that was written by Lieutenant Colonel Ollie North, when he was a White House aide for National Security and Ronald Reagan's liaison to FEMA – the Federal Emergency Management Agency. Rex 84 grew out of Iran-Contra, and permitted the federal government to suspend the Constitution, declare martial law, and detain any American deemed to be a national security risk.

Rex 84 and its successors, HSPD 51 and 20 scared the hell out of Pop. He knew from his history that Franklin D. Roosevelt had put more than 100,000 Japanese-Americans in "War Relocation" camps following the attack on Pearl Harbor (and a good thing that was, too, according to his grand pop, who thought that those interned represented a genuine threat to the nation). But now who knows who might be the target. All Pop knew was that the danger was real: hell, even that lefty, Naomi Wolf, who had been married to a Clinton speechwriter and told Al Gore to adopt a three-buttoned earth tone look during the 2000 presidential campaign, had written a book about the possibility of concentration camps and martial law. Pop thought that the very fact that someone on the left was willing to talk about it, was a sign that mischief was actually afoot.

About the only person he could talk about these things with was his old friend, KG. Certainly, none of the people he worked with gave a damn. KG thought that Rex 84 was the reason FEMA couldn't respond immediately to Hurricane Katrina: it was too busy setting up concentration camps.

***

Pop didn't work throughout the winter. He was eligible for unemployment compensation, but it didn't pay him enough to get his own place. He walked on tippy toes around Evelyn and Lou, who was now his mother's constant companion. In December, around Christmas time, Gran died. She looked shriveled and wrinkly in her coffin, like a plum that had been plucked from its tree too late and left out in the sun to rot. With her death, Pop felt like he was losing one of the last links to his own humanity; certainly, his continuum to the past was broken with her passing. He regretted that he hadn't asked her more about the olden days, or even her own family history. He wished he had taken the time to get to know who she was.

After the wake, mum went on a bender that lasted two, three, four, five days. Pop imagined all kind of scenarios to explain her absence, other than the obvious one that she was just on a drinking spree. He imagined that she and Lou had gone to Atlantic City and had drowned in the surf after falling off the boardwalk. Or that they had taken a barrel over Niagara Falls, like that couple he had heard about that took the plunge in a Kevlar-coated water tank and survived. Perhaps she was somewhere in South America with Josef Mengele. Pop could picture Evelyn and the Angel of Death dining on fava beans and liver with a nice Chianti at some street café in Buenos Aires, a scenario that was not very likely in real life, especially since Mengele had accidentally drowned while swimming in the Atlantic in 1979 at the ripe old age (from Pop's perspective) of 67. Now there's justice for you. There's another reason to believe in God.

Pop had nightmares about his mummy while she was gone. He dreamed that she was swimming in the dark in the Everglades when some beastly creature rose up out of a yellowish patch of moon glow and devoured her. He could almost hear her bones snapping and splintering in the creature's toothy mouth. In one of his dreams, mum was walking across some black and stumpy ground with grand pop and a man in a priest's collar before the three of them ignited in a flash. In another one of his dreams, Pop saw mum running through a field with a big white dog beside her. The dog became a powder puff, and later, a cloud that turned all dark and stormy and poured rain down upon her.

When mum returned, she announced that she and Lou had gotten married. There goes the inheritance, Pop thought. Not that there was much to inherit. Mum got the house they lived in from Gran when she died, but they didn't have much furniture, and what they had was vintage Texas Chain Saw Massacre, not made from bones exactly, but all spindly looking and crappy. Sugar Pop's old Buick had died shortly after he did, which was a plus because it probably saved Evelyn from another scrape with the law. (During her third DUI, she had collided with a parked car that just happened to be owned by a city detective. The incident cost her several nights in jail and a huge restitution payment). About the only thing of value in Mum and Pop's residence was the plasma TV Pop had paid nearly a grand for from his earnings at Brackenridge. Technically, it was his, but he wouldn't want to fight her for it, as it was the umbilical cord that connected her to the placenta of the American mass media, which enabled her to be conversant about the truly important issues of the day, like American Idol or Natalee Holloway or that woman who drowned her two sons in the lake and claimed that a black man did it (which even Pop, or especially Pop, had believed at the time.)

So Pop left the TV with her when he returned to work in the spring and his crew got assigned to a big renovation project near St. Mary's, Pennsylvania, about 125 miles away from Pop's home. St. Mary's was in Elk County, which lived up to its name. There were Elk Crossing signs everywhere, and Pop saw an elk – two actually – the first week he was there. He was driving up Winslow Hill near a town called Benezette when he saw a mother elk and her calf. He knew mom was an elk because she was bigger than a deer and her face was boxier, and she had a large round droopy nose rather than a pert little fawn-like one. Pop thought it might be fun to hunt elk, but his co-worker Sweeney told him it wouldn't be sporting. Unlike deer, Pennsylvania elk are acclimated to humans and haven't learned to perceive them as a threat. So it would be kind of like shooting fish in a barrel Sweeney said. Part of Pop understood what Sweeney was saying, but another part thought it might be swell to win a tag (Pennsylvania limited elk licenses and you have to enter your name in a drawing to get one) and see how many bulls one could take out – sort of like Cheney did when he killed all those ring neck pheasants in Ligonier when he was vice president.

Elk County was more than elk. There were towns nearby with American sounding names like Force and Rockton. Pop ended up getting himself a room over a bar in a town whose name wasn't quite as star spangled, but the price was right. The town was called Quayville, which was named after Matthew Quay, a Civil War Medal of Honor recipient and the man reputed to have fixed the 1888 presidential election, ensuring Benjamin Harrison's victory over Grover Cleveland. The town once depended on a paper mill to provide employment to the locals. (Paper from the mill was used by The Saturday Evening

Post during the days when Norman Rockwell did its covers.) Now, the mill was gone and the locals didn't do much of anything, except drink in the bar under Pop's apartment.

It was a rowdy place. People were always raisin' a ruckus. Country music poured out of the jukebox all damn day – and well into the night. Pop wasn't into country music. His own musical tastes had been conditioned by living in Florida, where he first learned about the Confederate Hammerskins and got to attend a hate rock concert in Ocala in the spring of 2006. That's when he got exposed to groups like Platoon 14 and Youngland, who were rock 'n rollers that sent up Country with tunes like "Thank God I'm a White Boy." (He picked up a Youngland CD for $5 and a Sniper Records T-shirt while he was there.) Personally, though, the further White Nationalist music, or WNist music, as it was called, was from Country, the better Pop liked it. He especially liked "Under the Hammer" by the WNist band Brutal Attack and "No More Brothers War" by Razor 88. He also was into black metal, digging songs like "Angry Mob Justice" by The Acacia Strain and "As I Lay Dying" by Nothing Left, which had a cool video that showed a woman being forced to walk a plank that jutted out from a mountain and that flash-repeated the phrase "Condemn the infected" every few seconds or so. Somewhat perversely, he also found himself attracted to Frank Lero's punk rock band Leathermouth. Lero, who was a pro-gay rights vegetarian (which meant, Pop guessed, that he couldn't suck himself off like he wanted to), had recorded a song "Catch Me If You Can," that likened the NYPD to Jack the Ripper. Lero also was, or had been, associated with a recording company named Skeleton Crew, which had a neat line of tee-shirts, including one that said "Kill Every Living Thing In Sight" and another that announced "I am a monster/Hate me/Destroy Me."

The problem with living over a bar was that it made it a hell of a lot harder to get up in the morning, which played into the antipathy his crew chief had toward him. Jack hated it when Pop was late. Whenever it happened, Jack would mother-fuck Pop until his face got blustery red (not the proverbial blue) and his veins would pop out of his temples and Pop thought he could literally see steam rising from Jack's flat-top. Pop paid a high price for Jack's rage. Whenever Pop was late, Jack would stick him with the shit jobs – outside work, working up on ladders, and lifting every fucking heavy thing Jack could find for him to lift. And, of course, Jack would dock his pay, conjuring memories of Pop's experience with Mr. Savage.

Sweeney, Edzel and Nixon didn't treat Pop any better, either, than they had the year before. It was still the same old you're-a-fuck-up-they-didn't-teach-you-anything-in-Florida shit from Sweeney. Edzel still thought Pop was stupid, and Nixon was still intent on belittling Pop for his sex life, or the complete lack thereof. The only thing different was that they tolerated Pop enough to drink with him, although, that perhaps may have had more to do with the fact that he lived over the only bar close to their work site.

One night, over shots and beers, Pop and Nixon got into it over politics. Unsurprisingly, Nixon was a very big Barack Obama supporter and had even done some canvassing for him during the Pennsylvania primary that

April. He tried to make it look like he was supporting him on some rational grounds, but Pop knew it was all or mostly about race.

Pop, on the other hand, hated Barack Obama. He thought he was unqualified – hell, he had only served one term in the Senate – and he didn't think he had much to offer, once you got past all his bullshit, the phony hope and change stuff.

He isn't qualified, you know, Pop said to Nixon.

What do you mean? Nixon said.

He doesn't have any experience.

Bullshit, Nixon told him. He was in the state senate in Illinois before he went to Washington.

He's the most unqualified person to run for President ever, Pop insisted.

He has about as much experience, maybe more, than Lincoln did, Nixon said.

And what did Lincoln do? Pop asked rhetorically. He screwed up the whole fucking country.

How, pray tell, did he do that?

Well, he freed the slaves for one thing.

I'm just going pretend I didn't hear that, Nixon said.

They drank silently for a while after that. Sweeney went to the bathroom and Edzel got up and put some money in the juke box, and Pop and Nixon tried not to look at each other while their two co-workers were gone. After Edzel sat down and Sweeney came back, Pop got up and went to the bar and got some tequila shooters. He gave one to Nixon – a gesture, sort of, of good will. Humpf, Nixon grunted, as Pop passed the shooter to him, but he didn't push the shot away. Pop watched while Nixon poured salt in the space between his forefinger and thumb. The salt crystals looked like little tiny shooting stars against the black background of his hand. Pop took the shaker and sprinkled some salt in the webbing of his own thenar space, the technical name for the place where the tequila salt goes (he had looked it up), and handed it to Sweeney, who followed suit, and passed it on to Edzel. When he was finished shaking, Edzel raised his shot glass and said salute.

The four of them simultaneously licked salt from their hands, drained their tequila shots, and bit into the lemon slices that were lying in front of them.

Yeehaw! Pop said when he was finished. Pop thought he heard Nixon sniff when he said, "Yeehaw," as if there was something offensive about the word. Don't you like my rebel yell? Pop wanted to say to him. Instead, he turned to Nixon and asked him if he thought Barack Obama was black enough.

Nixon gave him a sour look and it wasn't exclusively from the lemon. Black enough for what? he asked.

I don't know. I was listening to some dude on CNN the other day and he said Obama is having trouble convincing people in the black community that he's one of them. That's what the man said. He said Obama's got an Ivy League education and a Midwestern accent and his mother was, well, you know, white. Pop let the last word hang in the air, like one of those Goodyear blimps you see at sporting events before the violence starts. So some people, your people, apparently, don't think he's black enough, according to the man on CNN.

Well, let me ask you something, Nixon said, lighting a cigarette.

Sure, go ahead.

Pop thought Nixon was going to ask him if Obama was too black for him, if he thought his being African-American disqualified him from being president. (Pop would have said "yes." He was all for calling a spade a spade.) Instead, Nixon tried to lighten the conversation by smiling broadly, his teeth glistening in the darkness of the bar like pearls. "So," Nixon said, "you still ain't getting' any pussy, are you?"

Sweeney slapped his thigh. Edzel cackled. Pop felt his face turn red.

Why don't you ask your mother where she was last night? he said, his face still burning.

Oh, the white boy wants to do the dozens with me, eh, does he? Nixon said, rising from the table. He brought one of his hands up and touched Pop on the ear with it, as if he were Muhammad Ali extending a gloved hand to measure his opponent for a knockout punch. Well, the dozens is a game, he said, and the way I fuck yo momma is such a goddamn shame.

Ha, ha, Pop said. At least she doesn't do it for the money like yo momma.

Yo momma, Nixon said, is such a goddamn whore she got a 3-day waiting list.

Guys, guys, Sweeney said, as Pop got up on his feet and stood jaw to jaw with Nixon. The last sally had hit home, reminding Pop what a slut his mother was and sending his temperature spiking. He was still trying to come up with a good response to Nixon's jab when someone's elbow poked him in the ribs. Pop remembered reaching around Sweeney to get a piece of Nixon, who he assumed was the culprit. The next thing he knew, he was on the barroom floor. And Nixon was on top of him.

Get off, Pop bellowed.

I can't, Nixon answered, breathing hard. And it was true: the fat man couldn't lift himself up from the floor.

Get him off! Pop shouted to Sweeney, who had sat down on a chair next to the table and was rubbing the back of his arm.

Fuck you, Sweeney said, wincing in pain. Fuck the both of you.

Get him off! Pop yelled at Edzel, who was shifting his eyes back and forth from Sweeney to the pile-up on the floor.

Finally, some guys from the bar came over and helped Edzel hoist Nixon up and got Pop on his feet. He felt a crackling sensation in his right knee as he stood up, and he heard it snap and pop on him as he walked outside the bar. The sound reminded him of a log sizzling in a fireplace and the noise it makes when it burns.

The next morning, Pop's knee had swollen to nearly twice its normal size and he could barely stand to put any weight on it. He thought about calling off, but he knew he couldn't do it. Jack would can his ass. He was going to have to get through the day somehow. He didn't have an Ace bandage, so he took one of his tee-shirts (not the Sniper Records one) and ripped it in strips and wrapped them around his knee, tying them off tightly.

The knee still hurt like a sonuvabitch, and he thought he might have to hurl, the pain was that intense. Plus, he could scarcely bend his knee with his makeshift bandage on it.

Sweeney wasn't at work when he got there and limped into the place – Edzel said Sweeney's arm was bothering him pretty bad. That meant the three of them, Edzel, Pop and Nixon, had to do the work of four. Goddamn, Pop said to himself, but he tried to suck it up. It was hard, but he did what he had to do, minimizing exertion as much as he could, and trying to stay off of the knee. A couple of times, he put his weight down on it awkwardly and the pain shot all the way up to his jaw. He almost felt like crying, it was that bad.

They spent most of the morning cutting and framing windows on the east side of one of three interconnected buildings, and then Jack sent them over to the west side of the third building in the afternoon. Shit, Pop said, when he got the news they had to move. His knee gave out on him a couple of times as he walked there, and it got all crunchy and squishy on him when he sat down. It sounded like someone eating popcorn in a movie theater or munching on a big bowl of potato chips.

Pop figured that if he could hear the knee popping and crunching, somebody else could, too. And he was right. He saw Nixon looking at him as he was sitting on a piece of scaffolding. Pop was rubbing his sore knee pretty hard, and he thought he could see a smile curled on Nixon's face, the white of his teeth showing more than usual.

When they got to the west side, Nixon asked him if he had the router. No, I don't, Pop said. Edzel thought he had last seen it back on the other side of the complex, underneath a ladder sitting near a set of windows they had installed that morning. Nixon asked Pop to walk back there, to the east side of the complex, and retrieve it.

Why me? Pop asked him. You're the one who was

using it last.

Yeah, Nixon said, and you're the one who's going to walk over there and get it.

I don't understand, Pop said, balking at the request.

It's called seniority, Nixon told him. With Sweeny gone, I'm the senior man on the project today, and you're not.

Pop just sat there, fingers grooved in the articulations of his aching knee cap. He wasn't going anywhere, not then, no way, no how.

Let me put it to you in words you'll understand, Nixon told him. You're the nigga here.

Something snapped when Nixon said that, and it wasn't Pop's knee. He got up and walked toward Nixon, limping a little bit as he did. He had just got into a fighting stance when Jack came round a corner and asked him what the fuck he thought he was doing.

Nothin', Pop said.

Nothing my ass. I got one man off work because of the ruckus you caused last night, and now you're looking like you want to take out another one. Why don't you just turn in your tools and work boots and get the fuck out of here.

But, but, but, Pop sputtered. He wasn't sure who had told Jack about the incident last night, but he was sure he could guess. He, Pop said, pointing at Richard Nixon, was the one who started it.

I don't care who started it, Jack said. I'm finishing it. Like I told you, you're fired.

So, there's one set of rules for me, and a different set for him, Pop sputtered. He spat on the ground in the direction of Nixon's feet. Different rules for different fools, he muttered as he hobbled from the worksite.

Pop went back to Jack the next day and asked if he could have his job back. Look, Pop said, you're already a man down. Don't you need me? Jack folded his arms across his chest. I'm a man down with you or without you, he said.

Pop stayed in Quayville for a couple of days after he got fired. He didn't see any point in hurrying home. The last night he was there he went downstairs to the bar and sat in a corner booth all by himself and had a couple of beers. It was dark in the booth and he could barely read the menu the waitress had placed in front of him. It didn't matter. He wasn't hungry anyway.

Pop sipped his drink, and tried to keep his hands from shaking (the anger inside of him was that bad). What do you say? What do you know? What are you going to do? he asked himself. He was stuck in a country bar in the middle of nowhere and he was going nowhere, and getting there pretty fast. Pop felt a bitter taste in his throat, and it wasn't just from the beer. He daubed a finger at the tear that was just beginning to trickle down his face as the music blared out from the jukebox. The singer's voice twanged like a vibrating bow string after you let the arrow go, and the song she was singing was tinged with nostalgia and regret. For whatever reason, Pop remembered doing shots with Sugar the night he turned sixteen, and the shutter of his mental camera opened with a flash as his grandfather raised his shot glass in a salute to Pop. Liver spots dotted the back of Sugar's hand like speckles on the tail fin of a fish. These are the good ole days, young man, his grandfather told him with a wink. And you're really going to miss them once they're gone.

<u>KG</u>

Yesterday, after I came back from my shower, I took my tablet out of my box and was ready to take up my pen to begin writing again, but my flexi-pen wasn't with the tablet where I had left it. I thought perhaps that it had fallen to the bottom of the box and was hidden under some of my other things. So I very carefully emptied the box, removing my books, my shoes and underwear, my legal file, my bar of soap, the TP and my shower sandals (I had been given another pair after I complained about the sandal that was lost). I couldn't see the pen. I put my glasses on and took a closer look. Nothing. I turned the box upside down and tapped on it, but nothing fell out. I picked up the tablet again and rifled through it to make sure the pen wasn't rolled up in one of the pages. It wasn't.   I looked on my shelf and under the TV for my flexi-pen. It wasn't there. I got down on my hands and knees and looked under my cot for it. No luck. In virtual panic mode, I ran my hands over every inch of the floor of my cell, but didn't come up with anything. The pen wasn't in my cell. It wasn't just lost or missing. It was gone.

Obviously, someone had taken it.

At lunch, I asked the CO who gave me my lunch through the pie hole if he could ask if anyone had seen it, or, barring that, if he could get me a replacement, but he scarcely acknowledged me.

When he can back for my lunch tray, I asked him again.

No answer.

I asked for it again when a CO pushed my dinner tray through the pie hole, and I got the same silent treatment I had received before. I figured I would ask again when the CO returned and if I didn't get any satisfaction it would be the subject of my next phone call to Ronni Silverstein, whenever that would occur. Although I didn't have much of an appetite, I turned my attention to my dinner tray and suddenly noticed the flex-pen sticking out from my soft drink cup where a straw should have been.

Stop fucking with me, I said very loudly to the wall. Stop fucking with me, I screamed.

***

Seems like someone's always trying to fuck with me, Pop said to KG after he got home and told him how he had lost his job in Quayville. And this time, I really got fucked, Pop said, massaging his throbbing knee. It hurt like a bastard. Bu what really hurt was Pop's wounded ego. This was the second time he had been fired from a job, and he thought it was unfair. He thought it was especially unfair that he had been fired while Nixon kept his job. It's an affirmative action world, KG told him, where the average white guy always gets the shaft.

Pop and KG tended to agree on stuff. They had known each other for a long time -- since the second grade, in fact – and could almost read each other's minds, they knew each other that well. They met in the second grade and not sooner, because Pop had attended kindergarten and first grade at a different school than KG, a place called Phillip Murray Elementary, which was named after a Pittsburgh labor leader. (KG went to Arlington.) This was when Pop and mum were living in a housing project and before they moved in with Sugar and Gran and settled in KG's neighborhood.

The first time Pop saw Kenny he was catching fireflies in a jar in the early evening twilight. KG had poked holes in the jar lid so the fireflies could breathe after he caught them. Pop was interested in what the new boy was doing so he got his own jar, but he soon decided he would try to catch something bigger than a bunch of lightning bugs. Pop saw a blackbird sitting on a fence. He snuck up on it without spooking it and managed to get the blackbird in the jar with one panther-quick cupping move; unfortunately, he couldn't get the lid because the bird's belly was stuck in the circumference of the jar and its feet were sticking out of the jar's mouth, moving frantically. It's going to die, KG said to him. It can't breathe in there. Pop tried to shake the blackbird out of the jar. He couldn't. Kenny also tried to no avail. In a panic, Pop ran inside and got a hammer and came out and busted the jar open. It was too late to save the bird. Shards of glass lay all around its carcass. Blackbird, bye, bye, Kenny said.

Pop didn't know if it was because they had grown up together or what, but he and KG tended to see things the same way, almost as if they shared the same pair of eyes. (KG wasn't amblyopic, of course.) Both of them believed, for example, that African Americans got favorable treatment, and that Jews controlled the banking industry and Wall Street, and by extension, most of everything else. Over a beer one evening, KG speculated that African-Americans were descended from one of the lost tribes of Israel, and that was why the leaders of the American Zionist Owned Government, or ZOG, as he called it, tended to cut them a break through affirmative action in hiring and housing and other welfare programs. Pop thought KG's theory on this subject was inspired.

Why aren't we on the TV? Pop said after hashing out politics with KG. Why aren't we on radio? Hell, we make as much sense as Limbaugh or Hannity or O'Reilly or Levin or Savage, if not more than any of those guys.

That was probably where they should have left it.

But they didn't.

It was KG's idea. If Hal Turner could do it, he asked Pop, why the hell can't we?

Turner was a frequent caller to Sean Hannity's WABC radio talk show who started his own shortwave radio program before establishing himself as an internet talk radio host. Turner was one of the most brazen voices Pop and KG had ever heard. He once called for the assassination of a couple of federal judges, printing their names and addresses on his web site, and he reiterated Jefferson's comment that the Tree of Liberty occasionally needed to be watered with the blood of tyrants – a sentiment that especially appealed to Pop. But Hannity had thrown Turner under the bus after people asked him about their relationship in the midst of the flap over Obama's association with the Rev. Jeremiah Wright, an association Hannity had criticized, and later rumors surfaced that Turner was a paid FBI informant. The rumors prompted KG to walk back his enthusiasm for Turner, but only confirmed Pop's latent paranoia – ZOG wasn't above using agent provocateurs to entrap free men, but it could also bring a good man down by setting him up and making him look like a rat. The lesson, he guessed, was that you could never know exactly who to trust.

He nonetheless trusted KG's instinct on the radio program matter. Neither Pop nor KG knew much about shortwave or ham, but they readily agreed that the internet was the way to go. Pop dimly remembered that the FBI had shut down a low-frequency radio station operating from some guy's home in their neighborhood when Pop was a kid. He didn't know what the guy was doing or why it was perceived as a threat; he just knew that the Pittsburgh field office of the FBI didn't tolerate this mode of communication.

Their first order of business was to come up with a name and program format. They thought about calling their program "KG's Country," which was a play on "KD Country," an identifier of the Pittsburgh radio station KDKA, but Pop wasn't sure how "KG's Country" would appeal to the White Nationalist audience they were trying to attract, and KG thought Pop's name should be part of the program's title anyway. So they thought about "Pop and KG's Sweetalking Radio Hour," or Sweet Talk for short, but that didn't quite capture their political agenda (plus it sounded queer or black or both). KG liked "Voice of Amerika," but Pop thought it was a little bit too lefty sounding. For his part, Pop liked "Radiofreeamerica," the now defunct name of a right wing radio program operated by Tom Valentine on the Sun Radio Network in the 1990's, but it had a been there, done that kind of feel. They also thought about "Pop and KG's Straight Shootin' Radio Hour," but one of them (Pop wasn't sure who) shot that down. They nearly settled on "The Midnight Hour with Pop and KG," after the midnight ride of Paul Revere, then decided to go with "The Kenny and Pop Show," which was a throwback to "The Opie and Anthony Show" which they had loved when they were younger, but had nothing at all to do with politics. (Opie and Anthony had a program on XM Satellite Radio where they once did a bit, called "Sex for Sam," offering Samuel Adams beer to anyone who had sex in a notable public place. The bit ended after a Virginia couple got caught having sex in a vestibule of St. Patrick's Church Cathedral in Manhattan, and Opie and Anthony got fined $357,000 by the FCC.)

As for format, they broke it down into four fifteen-minute segments. "There was "Pop Kulture," also to be known as "Issue Du Jour," where Pop would give his take on the issues of the day, and "Pop Music," of course, where Pop intended to play the kind of music he liked. There was "Smooth Talk with Kenny G," where KG got to say whatever he wanted, and "The Outer View," where Pop and KG intended to do interviews of people with new and different points of view, or even ordinary people who did something to protect their race or to keep the blacks and Jews in check.

They launched in June, right after Obama had sewn up the Democratic Party nomination. They recorded their show from the basement of Kenny's home, and uploaded it to the web using a service that charged them $39 a month. They found that they didn't have enough content to fill up a whole hour, so their first program was just ten minutes long and was padded with some audio and video clips they downloaded from the internet. The show began with a few seconds of a song called "D J Culture" by the Pet Shop Boys that sounded like black metal at the beginning but soon devolved into something really gay, or so Pop thought. KG liked the song because it had secret messages encoded in French (which Pop also thought was really gay.) They replaced the music for their second show, and after that Pop wouldn't let KG have any input into the selections.

In the first show, Pop did a rant about Barack Obama that he thought was pretty tame, but that was liberally sprinkled with the N-word. KG told him not to do it. He was pretty sure it violated their terms of use, which prevented them from posting, storing, transmitting or disseminating anything that was unlawful, threatening or defamatory, libelous, or obscene. Pop didn't think it was any of those things, although he did allow that it was one of those words, maybe the only word, that you couldn't say in public, unless, of course, you happened to be black, and then you could get away with it. You could say all seven of the dirty words that George Carlin said you couldn't say on television in 1972, including "shit," which was spoken in several episodes of NYPD Blue, and "fuck," which got broadcast during a CBS documentary on 9/11, and wasn't bleeped out and was now all over cable 24/7. You could say the seven dirty words and even George Carlin's expanded canon of 200 dirty words, which included expressions like "merkin" and "quim" and "yodeling in the gully," but you couldn't say the N-word, which didn't even make George Carlin's list (you can look it up). Hell, even Mark Twain's Huckleberry Finn, which was an American literary classic, was third or fourth on the list of most-banned books because it used the N-word more than 200 times. Pop predicted the day would come when you wouldn't be able to read Huck Finn in the original version, only in an edited one that culled out every mention of the N-word, but why would you want to bother with a book that made a hero of a black man anyway?

For the second show, Pop dialed it back. He gave some commentary on the Supreme Court's decision in McDonald v. Chicago, which held that the Second Amendment right to bear arms applied to the individual states. Pop thought the Court wimped out. First, the decision didn't explicitly overrule the City of Chicago's ban on handguns, which was at issue in the case, although most commentators were viewing it that way. Second, and more insidiously, the decision left the door open to state and local firearms regulation. Pop's commentary lasted all of six minutes, which was long enough to put his friend to sleep, not to mention all those people out there on the web that Pop and Kenny were trying to reach. Although they did the program in real time and invited listeners to call in, they didn't get a single response. Pop thought they needed to step it up a bit, show a little more nerve, and restoke the enthusiasm of their initial broadcast.

Pop thought he found his métier on the third show. First he got himself a skinhead haircut so he could look more the part of the talk show host he wanted to be. (His mother's new husband didn't like it, about which we will have more to say later.) Pop also got a tattoo. He got himself an Americanized version of the Iron Eagle, the

Nazi symbol of an eagle suspended over the swastika. Pop's version used an American Bald Eagle, and it didn't have a swastika. It was colored red, white and blue, and the eagle's wings spread out across his chest. The eagle's head was right below the collar line, and the tattoo was visible whenever Pop unbuttoned his shirt a couple of buttons down. Everyone Pop knew (which was only Kenny) liked it, except for Pop's stepfather (who could just fuck off) and probably his mother, who had a small tattoo of a dolphin on her ankle and seemed to be oblivious to the tattoo on her son's chest.

Second, Pop decided to go with some racier material. His topic du jour was the Virginia Tech mass killings, which had happened in April 2007 but were recently in the news again with the announcement of an $11 million court settlement in a suit against the Commonwealth of Virginia brought by some of the victims' families. The killings had been perpetrated by a South Korean named Seung-Hui Cho, who killed 32 people and wounded 25 others in the deadliest shooting incident by a single gunman in U.S. history.

Even though Cho was a slope-eyed gook who should never have been allowed in the country, he engaged some of Pop's sympathy. First, there was something about Cho that reminded Pop of his grand pop (perhaps the fact that they both were functionally autistic, or maybe it was just that Cho tapped Pop's memories of Sugar's memories of living in Asia. Are your memories of someone else's recollections truly your own?) Second, there was a tangential Pittsburgh connection between Virginia Tech and Cho. Cho's English Department chairman, who once offered the troubled student tutorial help, had a code word that was to prompt her assistant to call the police if she felt threatened by the student. The code name happened to be the last name of her predecessor as chairman, a former Carnegie Mellon University professor and English Department head.

Mostly, however, Pop felt sympathy toward Cho because the senior English major had been harassed by the Virginia Tech faculty, including that N-word Nikki Giovanni, who threw Cho out of her poetry class and said she would resign if he were allowed back in. Her problem with her student: he wore round, mirrored John Lennon-type sunglasses to school and a cap pulled down over his ears and face and didn't like to speak in class because he was self-conscious. So the Distinguished Professor of English Literature, who had written a poem called "The True Import of Present Dialogue," which included such lines as, "Do you know how to draw blood/Can you poison?/Can you stab-a-Jew/Can you kill, huh?" and, "Can you piss on a blond head/Can you cut it off/Can you kill a white man?" deemed him to be dangerous and chucked him out of class. This insult was repeated by some of Cho's other professors, who dumped on him in class and generally treated him like a pariah, and one whom even forwarded Cho's allegedly "blood-drenched" writings to the Virginia Tech police (who didn't do anything about it, perhaps because Cho's poems and stories weren't that blood-drenched at all, or not as blood-drenched as the work of his professors).

In short, Cho had been mobbed. Pop knew what it was like to be mobbed, because he had just recently undergone the experience in Quayville.

Pop used some black metal music to introduce his

on-air rant about Cho and the Virginia Tech shootings. He was a couple of minutes into it when he had a Hal Turner moment. Pull the trigger, he said, reliving Cho's acts of violence. Pull the fucking trigger, he screamed. All he has to do is pull the trigger and POW! ... thirty-two fucking people dead. I'm righteously impressed with that ... thirty-two, thirty-three people dead, including Cho himself. That's fucking doomsday status.

Then Pop popped ripped open his shirt, exposing the Iron Eagle on his chest, and turned to face the camera squarely and said, "I want to kill my ex-girlfriend. I want to kill her mother. I want to kill my mother. I want to kill my father and my stepfather. I want to kill everyone that I don't like, and, in a random measure, I'd like to take out a couple of members of the Pittsburgh police force, too, or maybe even a couple of FBI agents, or Treasury, or the goddamn Secret Service, anyone who helps to keep the ZOG in power."

Well, that'll get us thrown off the air, for sure, KG said when Pop was done.

But it didn't.

What brought the program to an end was Kenny's father, who didn't like what they were doing in the basement, and especially didn't like it when they played their black metal music loud, and hated it even more when they did not, because when they were too quiet he thought they might be doing something queer, giving each other hand jobs maybe, or sucking each other off. Pop took umbrage with that and wanted to call Kenny's dad out, but KG begged him not to. I don't want him to kick me out.

KG's dad banned them from the basement of his house

in August, a few days before the Republican National Convention was to convene. Pop and KG planned to watch the convention, which they had once hoped to blog about, from Junior Olup's bar, where they went for old times' sake. It wasn't Olup's anymore. A couple of lesbians had bought it, and were trying to remake the place into a dyke hangout. Pop and KG snickered loudly when the dyke bartender served them drinks, and snickered a little more when Sarah Palin appeared on the TV screen over the bar, introducing herself as a gal from the North Slope of Alaska. (Something about the word "Slope" struck them as darn funny. Maybe it was the context. Maybe it was because of where they were.) Palin kept making reference in her acceptance speech to all the kids she had birthed on her way to becoming governor of the most frigid state in the union, and Pop and KG clapped every time she mentioned one of her offspring. All the lesbians in the place were staring glumly at their drinks as Palin's image flickered on the TV screen, just waiting, Pop and KG figured, for the Alaskan governor to start telling them they were inauthentic Americans and that the Lesbian-Gay-Bisexual-Transgendered Axis of Evil was bringing the country down. Pop and KG cheered Palin so loudly they were asked to leave the bar (in a polite lesbian sort of way). They went across the street to C J's, a blue collar bar, where the only women in the place were a couple of floozies, getting there just in time to see McCain come to the podium.

Pop had never been much of a McCain fan. He didn't think he was a true hero and privately believed that McCain had collaborated with Hanoi, revealing military information to protect his own skin while he was a POW. He also hadn't liked McCain's prosecutor-like questioning of Dolores Alfond at a hearing before a Senate committee on MIAs – Alfond's brother, a pilot like McCain, had been shot down over North Vietnam and then went missing, a fact that hardly mattered to the senator, who treated Alfond like shit, calling her a liar and getting up and stomping out like a petulant child in the middle of her testimony. No, if you asked Pop, John McCain was a sellout. The only good thing Pop could say about him was that he had picked Palin, the most genuinely real person (the real-ist?) he had seen in politics in his life (and the only candidate he had ever wanted to fuck). Pop especially liked it when Palin got all "mavericky" (to use her phrase) on the campaign trail, and there were nights when he cuddled up with his Maverick (the Mossberg) in his bed and thought fondly of her. (Palin made him glad that he bought the Maverick rather than holding out for a Mossberg 500 or 590, even though they were reputed to be better than the model he got.) Truth be told however, Pop couldn't vote for Palin if she were running for president instead of VP. He didn't think a woman should be president (hell, America wasn't Israel or Britain or India or Pakistan, where any dumb broad could end up in charge), just as he wasn't ready for a black man in the oval office. (As much as Pop was a fan of Clarence Thomas, he didn't think there automatically had to be a black seat on the Supreme Court, either; he also thought Thomas' appointment was a Republican form of affirmative action, affirmative action in principle if it wasn't affirmative action in name.) In fact, Pop was troubled by people like Michael Steele and Bobby Jindal, who were the new faces of the Republican Party (which seemed to put anyone with a vagina or a face darker than a paper bag into a leadership post.) There was something about the Republican faces of diversity that made him wonder if the party had been taken over by Democrats. It was a question he would have liked to have posed on his and KG's Internet radio show, if KG's father hadn't shut the program down.

They had tried taking the show to Pop's house, but that didn't work out either. Lou and Evelyn were always home (neither of them worked), and Evelyn would get on Pop's ass about doing chores, and Lou would get on his ass about practically everything. (He thought his marriage to Evelyn gave him the right to boss Pop around.) Lou didn't like Pop's political views (he had once been on the City payroll and was a lifelong Democrat), or his religious views (Lou was a diehard Catholic, not that it kept him from breaking church rules all the time, like taking the Lord's name in vain and drinking and coveting his neighbor's new sedan and drinking and committing blasphemy against the spirit and drinking and walking around the house in his underwear and drinking and … . (In Lou's defense, he was adamantly opposed to abortion.)

The one thing Lou particularly did not like was Pop's friendship with KG. Lou thought they egged each other on, and that their relationship would eventually land them both in trouble. Consequently, Lou would try to jack them off every chance he got, calling them names like "Bonnie and Clyde," which should have earned him a shiner, or "Fugate and Starkweather," or even "Smith and Hickock." Pop knew who Starkweather was from the Springsteen album, Nebraska," but he didn't know who Smith and Hickock were. What's more, he didn't like the way their names rolled off his stepfather's lips. Once, when he was in an especially combative mood, he challenged Lou about it. What the fuck are you calling me and KG? Pop asked. Who are these Smith and Hiccup fuckers?

There were a couple of boys who hung out together and talked tough and whose tough talk got them hanged after they talked each other into robbing some farmer in Kansas and didn't get anything and ended up killing the farmer and his family. Truman Capote wrote about them in the book, In Cold Blood.

Well I don't know anything about the Coyote book, Pop said, intentionally mispronouncing the author's name, and I know even less about these Smith and Hickock fucks, but that ain't me and KG. So, I'd appreciate it if you'd stop comparing me and KG to them, or to Bonnie and Clyde, either, and if you do, I'll stop comparing you and Evelyn to Gomez and Morticia or Clarice and Hannibal or a couple of fucking clownfish.

Point taken, Lou said.

Point, game, set, match.

Later Pop read the Capote book, but he wasn't impressed with it. It was full of all kind of psychologizing about the minds and motives of two killers. Like all the famous pairs of men in American literature – Huck and Jim, Natty Bumppo and Chingachgook, Ishmael and Queequeg, Nick and Gatsby, Tonto and the Lone Ranger Perry Smith and Richard Hickock were locked in a subconsciously homoerotic relationship, a pair of men seeking to flee for the primal wilderness rather than remain in the domesticating world of women, but ending up in dystopian Kansas instead. (That at least was the assessment Pop read on the internet in one of those synopses readers post on Amazon. Pop didn't quite know what it meant, but he liked the sound of it.) In any event, he was sure that Coyote didn't know anything. For example, he called Hickock an ephebophile, which is a fancy term for someone who is attracted to girls between the ages of 15 and 19, and claimed that his partner prevented him from raping the farmer's daughter, who was sixteen year old. But most men, Pop included, are attracted to teenage girls (the younger the better, he and KG snickered), and it doesn't mean that they are pervs. (Truth be told, Pop not only liked young women, like Keilah, but also liked older ones, like Kathy, too, as long as they were hot – is there anything perverted about that?) As for Smith, the author was clearly hypnotized by him and in some gay trance that prevented him from seeing Smith clearly or understanding what he was about. In the last analysis, Pop had to agree with that homosexual Tom Wolfe (anyone who wears a white suit all the time like Wolfe does and Capote did when he was researching In Cold Blood either has to be gay or terminally affectatious) when he called the Capote book "pornoviolence," neither a "who-done-it" nor a "will-they-be-caught," but just a screed promising gory details and withholding them, like a squirt up the ass, until the very end (no pun intended). Like most of what gets written nowadays, it was a faggot's view of the world.

Stepdada

I haven't written a word in a month, a relatively short time I guess for someone on the outside, but a long time in here, where life is so interminable that, to paraphrase the poet, Blake, you can hold your dick in your hand for an eternity but you ain't ever, ever going to get laid. I had just mailed off the last chapter of this book to my lawyer, the one about Pop and the blackbird and him and KG on the internet, and had started in on another. Then I went to the law library for a scheduled hour of research, and came back to find that my manuscript was gone, along with my writing tablet and my pen.

When I complained about it to the COs, I was told that my writing contained information that might jeopardize the security of the prison.

Like what? I asked. Like how you guys need to have to put your noses up my ass every time I enter and leave my cell? How does that jeopardize the vaunted security of the prison?

No one had an answer, but one of the COs allowed that the warden was concerned about all the "neo-Nazi hate stuff" in my book and my almost continual use of the N-word.

I complained about it to Ronni Silverstein the next time I saw her. In fact, I was so fixated on the issue that I completely forgot that there was a woman on the other side of the glass, and I never once asked her to unbutton her blouse so I could see her tits, or to pull her skirt up so I could see her panties. I don't think she was too interested in my problem (I think she had read the chapters I sent her, and wasn't too impressed, especially with the anti-Semitic parts) but she said she'd look into it for me and see what she could do to redress my grievance with the prison.

It took a month, but I got my stuff back, the tablet and the pen anyway. Fortunately, most of what I had written is still rolling around in my head, and I think I'll be able to recreate what was lost.

Personally, I don't think the censorship and stealing of my writing had anything to do with the warden at all. I just think one of the COs was fucking around with me. And I'm sure he'll do it again.

***

This is a Cristal Stick Ball pen, medium point, blue, with the clear plastic housing removed and no iconic streamlined cap. This is a recycled Composition Notebook 69C sold in the U.S.A. by some Chinese paper products manufacturer through its German distributor. This is Pop with the pen in his hand and the notebook on his lap, trying to get back into his novel. This is me, sitting on my ass on the prison cot that will be my bunk for the rest of my fucking life. (Well you've made your bed, so sleep in it, buddy.) I feel encouraged to go on.

Pop spent the second November in Tuesday glumly

watching TV as the election returns came in. The polls closed in Pennsylvania at 8:00 p.m. EST, and NBC declared Obama the winner of the state at 9:20 p.m. Pop's stepfather, Lou, was ecstatic, and told his stepson so. He can't lose now, stepfather said. Then Indiana and Virginia went south for McCain, metaphorically speaking, and all of the major networks called the race for Obama at 11:00 p.m.

Well, Pop thought, as he saw his mother and stepfather hugging in front of the TV screen (two racists cheering the election of a black man, who'd have thunk it?), this is the triumph of ordinary people in extraordinary times – times that cried out for something truly remarkable and wonder-making and not what we were getting. Like Obama, Pop's stepfather was common and low bred, undistinguished in appearance, with no achievements in his past that heralded the exceptional in the future. Lou had a regular men's haircut, battleship gray hairs decking his temples and a thinning shock of gray hair mopping across his forehead. He had a mesorrhine Slavic nose (Lou Wisniewski was Polish), a strongly built jaw, and tits so big he needed a shoulder boulder holder, a Frank Costanza manssiere. He also had a large paunch around his waist (his "Iron City beer belly," he called it), his heavy upper torso supported by two stork-like legs. Pop thought he was a heart attack waiting to happen, and he just couldn't wait for Lou's heart attack to occur.

Lou Wisniewski was known by his friends as "the Wizard," or, simply as "the Wiz." Pop hardly ever called him that. (He derisively referred to him as "whizz" or "whizzer" a few times when Lou got up to take a pee.) Befitting his nickname, Lou was a congenital know-it-all who had an opinion about everything. He had political opinions ("O-ba-ma! O-ba-ma!") and religious ones (The Pope was always right.) Lou's political opinions and religious ones were sometimes irreconcilable, but the Wiz wasn't wizardly enough to resolve, or even recognize, the conflict. (What does the Pope think about the Democratic Party's plank on abortion? Pop taunted him. What about stem-cell research?) The Wiz had opinions about sports (The Steelers were the greatest football team ever, and the Pirates and Penguins were just attention placeholders until football season came around again.) He truly believed the music ended when Buddy Holly, Ritchie Valens and The Big Bopper died, and didn't know a damn thing about rock and roll, or any other music genre, after 1959. Lou loved Elvis, Chuck Berry, and Bill Haley and the Comets, but he didn't give a whit for anyone after that. Not the Beatles, not the Stones, or any other band most other old geezers rolled out for in their American flag shirts and leather pants and 60's hairdos at the old rocker concerts at Heinz Field and the First Niagara Pavilion. ("The First Viagra Pavilion," Pop called it.)

Lou had a relative on the County Democratic Committee who got him a clerical job with the Prothonotary. ("What the hell is a prothonotary?" Harry Truman asked during a campaign stop in Pittsburgh in 1948. The prothonotary, or the pro, as the Wizard called him, was the chief clerk of the civil court.) Lou worked for the prothonotary all his life, leaving the position for an early retirement after his ticker started acting up. He spent his retirement years at the Lyceum, a local bar, except for a few months in the winter when he went to Florida. Pop's mum met him at the bar, where Lou bought her a drink, the functional equivalent, for Evelyn, of love.

As far as Pop and Lou were concerned, it had been hate since first sight. The first time Pop saw Lou he was pawing up his mummy on the couch. The first time Lou saw Pop he was a dependent adult male child interrupting his coitus. It was strictly downhill from there.

I don't like your haircut, Lou said to Pop after Pop came home with his skinhead cut.

I don't like it that you're fucking my mother, Pop replied.

I don't like the tattoo, Lou said after Pop came home with an Americanized iron Eagle splayed across his chest.

I don't like it that you're fucking my mother, Pop replied.

I don't like your friend Kenny, Lou said, after Pop brought a high and inebriated KG home for dinner one evening.

I don't like it that you're fucking my mother, Pop replied.

Pop's responses to Lou had a repetitious quality.

Pop thought Lou was way too old for his mother. It was like her dating her father, for Christsake. From Pop's perspective, it was even worse than Evelyn dating Ray, even though Evelyn and Lou weren't related. It was "symbolic incest," goddamn it, Pop said to KG.

KG told Pop to chill. They probably don't have sex very often at their age.

Once is too much for me, Pop said. And he meant it.

Thus Pop entered his Hamlet phase. He started to wear black, putting away his sage green MA1-flight jacket, "Emo Sucks" tee-shirts, ¾ inch burgundy clip-on suspenders (Saul Savage would have been proud) and 501 jeans with the cuffs rolled up over his steel-capped grinders (Pop's skinhead wardrobe, Lou called it.) In its place, Pop adopted more of a Goth or Goth punk look: a black leather vest worn over a black gas station tee-shirt with a red, white and blue Tri-Star Red Hat logo on the front, black Asylum junkie fit bondage pants with snaps on the pockets and buckles up and down the legs, and vintage black motorcycle boots. (To pay for his new clothes, Pop sold the Taurus 24/7 .45 caliber pistol with the Novak self-luminous night sight he had purchased in St. Mary's right before he got fired.) He also let his hair grow out, wearing it in a devilock style, the sides and the back still short, but the front long and worn forward. Lou, who hadn't liked Pop's baldy style of haircut hated his devilock even more. It makes you look like Eddie Munster, Lou told him.

Pop thought he was making a politico-fashion statement (his phrase). Lou thought he was making an ass of himself (his exact words). To punctuate his statement for his stepfather, Pop took off his gas station tee and replaced it with one that said "McCain Palin '08" (this was before black Tuesday, as Pop later referred to election day). The tee was black, of course. That's great, that's really great, Lou said when he saw it. How many votes do you think you're taking away from McCain and swinging to Obama when you wear that? Pop thought about what Lou said and (begrudgingly) decided that he may have a point. So he started to alternate the McCain Palin tee with one that said "Nobama." After a while, it became the one that he liked best.

The problem of what to do with Lou became his consuming project that fall. He had overheard Lou talking to mummy through the wall that separated their bedroom from his: Stepfather clearly wanted him out of the house. He would have been gone, too, he was sure of it, were it not for his knee, and the tiny smidgen of sympathy he garnered for it. The swelling had gone down considerably but the knee still clicked when he walked, and there were times when it occasionally went out on him. He had lost his Access Card and county Medicaid when he went to work in St. Mary's, and he didn't have private health insurance. Once, when the knee was really bothering him, he went to the Emergency Room of a local hospital. The E.R. doctor told him he had probably torn his meniscus. He got an x-ray at the E.R., but it didn't show anything, and the doctor told him he should probably get an M.R.I. scan and see a specialist. But Pop didn't have the money, so he had to live with the pain. His pain and discomfort was noticeable, too, noticeable enough for even Evelyn to comment that his knee must be really bothering him. That was nice, that Evelyn cared enough to notice. Pop credited the sympathy factor for his being allowed to stay. Plus, mum still harbored some residual sentiment in his favor because he had cared for her in her recovering alcoholic phase, right before her total relapse. (Oh, what times they had! Oh, how they bonded! Memories of The Jerry Springer Show flooded over him, misting him to tears. Je-rry! Je-rry! Je-rry! Hours of your life you'll never get back. Pop thought he and Evelyn and Lou would make for a great Jerry Springer episode. In fact, he imagined one called "Avenging Stepsons" in which he got to throw a chair at Lou on stage and that ended with him getting bussed on the cheek by one of the show's three female security guards – he liked Mimi Madrigal the best because she reminded him of Keilah.)

In his spat with Lou, Pop had more going for him than Evelyn's residual affection for her son. Kicking Pop out of the household was Lou's idea, not Evelyn's. Yes, it had been mum's idea not too far back, but she had forgotten that. Now, it was Lou's axe to grind, which meant that Pop had Evelyn's contrarian nature going for him rather than against him. He knew from long experience that any idea that wasn't Evelyn's was doomed from the very outset. His problem was what to do with Lou in the meantime. He wanted his stepfather out of the proverbial picture, wanted him out of the household just as surely as Lou wanted him gone. Pop knew that Lou's leaving was an eventual certainty, as close as one could get to an Eternal Verity, in fact. With the possible exception of Pop himself, no man could live with mum for more than a couple of months, not even with the benefit of legal sedation or illegal substances. The problem was that once Lou was gone no one was going to serve as a buffer between Evelyn and Pop.

Pop experienced leviathan cognitive dissonance and Hamlet-like indecision. He thought about killing his stepfather, of course, capping him in the head with the Bersa he still packed most days. He thought about shooting him with his Mavericky shotgun, too, particularly in those moments when Lou was crowing about Obama. But that wouldn't have done it. In reverse Hamlet fashion, he wanted to kill his stepfather while he was at prayer. (Pop was unconcerned that Lou might go to heaven if he capped him while he was on his knees worshiping; he also thought it would make more of a statement, one that would give the Catholic League something to think hard about.) The problem with this scenario was that it involved witnesses as the only time that Lou Wisniewski prayed was when he was at church. Pop wished that his stepfather was more of an evangelical, one who prayed in public constantly, like those fools one saw at the corner of Smithfield and Fifth Avenue all the time, screaming "Jay-sus!" and handing out leaflets to anyone who passed by.

Sunday mass was the only time Lou Wisniewski wasn't with Pop's mummy. Lou and Evelyn drank together at the Lyceum most mornings, they watched TV most afternoons from the couch, and they returned to the Lyceum most evenings for a toddy or two or three or four before retiring to the master bedroom, where they often took a bottle with them, one of Evelyn's BIG bottles of vodka or gin. As close as they were, as intimately as they shared each other's space, they did not go to mass together. Evelyn drew the line at religious devotion and display. She didn't feel the need for religious inspiration. Shit, if she wanted inspiration, she could reach for the top-shelf stuff. Evelyn also didn't feel the need to confess her sins. Hell, if she wanted confession, she didn't need a priest – she had her bartender.

Pop followed Lou to mass and back a couple of Sundays. Lou was a creature of routine. He always drove the same route. Down Cologne to Salisbury, turn left on Fernleaf, up the hill to the Avenue, take another left, and park behind the old trolley stop, where the steel tracks for the trolley were still visible, just across the street from

St. Henry's Church. It was just a five minute drive, hell, the Wiz could have walked it if he wasn't so effin' fat. Despite the brevity of the distance, so to speak, Pop figured that if he wanted to clock his stepfather, there were a couple of places along the way where he could pull up alongside Lou's battered old Cadillac, and fire away. Shit, if he clocked him on the Avenue, people would probably blame it on some black kid from the Projects. The problem was that Lou tended to go to mass at noon, rather than at 6 or 8 or 10, and there were more people out on the streets at that time. If Pop plugged Lou before or after the noon Sunday mass, there was a good chance someone would see it.

There were a couple of times when he half-decided to do it, notwithstanding the risk. After he let his hair grow out (on top and in the front anyway) Pop had begun to feel like Travis Bickle (without the Mohawk, of course). He didn't drive a cab and wasn't into hidden spring-loaded holsters like Bickle was (Pop liked to carry his Bersa tucked inside his waistband rather than up his sleeve), but he found himself practicing a tough-guy swagger in front of his bedroom mirror, sneering "You talkin' to me? You talkin' to me? " to the image staring back. The Travis Bickle in him wanted to snuff Lou Wisniewski. The only thing holding him back was opportunity.

One evening, not too long after Obama was elected, Lou and Evelyn had a fight. Pop didn't know exactly what had prompted it, only that Evelyn had stormed out. He half expected Lou to run after her, but his stepfather didn't. Lou just poured himself a stiff one, eased himself into the recliner and turned on the TV set. He watched a little CNN and then he tuned in his favorite program,

Countdown with Keith Olbermann. C'mon, c'mon, he motioned to Pop when Pop came out of his room to get something to drink from the kitchen, a trajectory that required him to pass by Lou's chair. C'mon, c'mon, get a glass and sit with me, Lou said, as he picked up his bottle of Jack, indicating that he would be happy to share it with his stepson if he grabbed a chair and pulled it up. Pop's first instinct was to pass. He liked Jack Daniels, but he hated Keith Olbermann. In fact, he perhaps hated him even more than the President-Elect. Olbermann was … well just fill in the blank. Jack or Keith? It was a real Approach-Avoidance conflict.

Fortunately, or unfortunately, as the case may be, Olbermann wasn't doing his show that night. Dave Shuster was filling in. Pop didn't have quite as much of an axe to grind with Shuster as he did with Olbermann. So he pulled up a chair and sat down next to his stepfather.

Lou Wisniewski poured Pop a drink. A big one. Considerably more than three fingers. Pop said thanks, and sipped from his glass.

No, no, don't sip it, Lou said. Chug it. Chug it back.

An obedient stepson, Pop did what he was told.

Lou poured him another one.

On the TV screen, which didn't seem quite in focus despite the 1080i resolution of its plasma screen, Dave Shuster and Chuck Todd were jawing about the Senate Democratic Caucus vote to keep Joe Lieberman as chairman of the Homeland Security Committee.

Pop took a big gulp of his Jack and leaned in toward Lou. So how's that "Change You Can Believe In" thing going for you now?

They had to do it, Lou said. He's the 60th vote in the

Senate chamber.

Well, I'm glad it isn't politics as usual, Pop said. He took another big gulp from his glass, and asked Lou if he minded hitting him again.

Lou poured some more Jack into Pop's glass.

Shuster was playing Odd Ball. One of the features was a World Dominos Day Event in which some 4 million plus dominos were toppled. Kind of like the U.S. now, after Obama, Pop wanted to say. But he didn't. Instead, he leaned forward and asked Lou: Doesn't Obama's appointment of Geithner and Summers and soon-to-be secretary of state Hilary Clinton bother you?

No, no, Lou said. I'm sure Barack knows what he's doing. He's building a team of rivals, he said.

On the TV screen, Shuster was talking about the upcoming coronation. Four million people – about the number of those falling dominos – were expected to show up in Washington when Barack Obama took the Oath of Office. Shuster was saying that it would make Obama's election night victory speech, which had a crowd of 200,000, look like a tea party. (And, oh, how that resonates now.)

Pop asked Lou if he had received his ticket to the Inaugural Ball.

Lou said that because he was a contributor to the campaign, he expected that he would receive an invitation to come to the Mall to hear the presidential inauguration speech. It may not be a ball, he said, but it would still be something, and he was actually thinking about going.

You're kidding, Pop said, as he chugged back his glass of Jack.

No, I'm really serious Lou told him.

You'd drive all the way to Washington to see that nigger take the Oath of Office? Pop asked as he held out his glass for more Jack.

He's not a nig ..., Lou said, stopping himself before he could complete the word. He's your President. And I think you've had enough to drink.

He isn't my president, Pop said, as he put down his glass and got up from his chair. He put his hands down on the arms of the chair to steady himself as he rose. Once he was on his feet, he turned to walk away from Lou and back into his room, but something tugged him back. Maybe it was the annoyance he felt over being refused another drink. Or maybe it was just their whole goddamned stupid conversation that had got his goat. In any event, Pop turned and faced his stepfather. Lou was pouring himself another stiff one from his bottle of Jack. Pop waited until his stepfather was finished pouring. Hey, Lou, he said as he pulled the handgun from his waistband and pointed it at the bridge of Lou Wisniewski's nose.

<u>MIA/404</u>

Where's Lou? Mum asked when she came home.

I dunno, Pop said. Wasn't he with you?

No, he stayed home when I went out. Didn't you see him?

No, I didn't mum, Pop said. I spent most of the evening in my room

You spend too much time on the internet, mum scolded. Then, after a pause, where do you think he went?

Haven't a clue, mum. Sorry.

Do you think he went to the Lyceum?

You were there, weren't you? You'd have seen him.

Maybe he went to Stan's Café?

Not very likely. He hates the crowd at Stan's.

Yeah, but if he was trying to avoid me, he may have gone to Stan's. Maybe I should go there and look?

It's after closing time, mum. They won't let you in.

You really haven't seen him?

No, mum, I haven't.

Mum sat up for a little while smoking cigarettes at the kitchen table. The smoke formed a thick haze that reminded Pop of a dirty white cat; the creature arched its cloud back against the ceiling while its fog belly hung over the table. The smoke stung Pop's eyes and aggravated his amblyopia, causing him to see double. Two chain-smoking whiskey drinking floozydressed Evelyns were too much for him. Excusing himself, Pop went to his room, lay down on the bed and closed his eyes. He could feel his heart banging in his chest. He tried not to think about the day. He tried not to think about what the future had in store for him. He tried not to think. Eventually, his heart stopped clattering, its pace becoming more metronomic, and Pop drifted off to sleep.

In the night, he felt someone tugging at his sleeve.

Pop unlidded an eye and looked up at his mother. She had changed out of her floozy dress into a pink bathrobe.

What time is it? Pop asked.

It's three a.m., mum said, and I'm really worried. Lou's not home, and his car isn't in the driveway. Maybe he was in a wreck?

You'd know, mum, if that'd happened you'd have got a call.

Maybe he drove off the road and he's lying in a ditch in the dark and no one knows he's there.

Mum, you're being paranoid, Pop said.

An hour later, Pop felt another tug at his sleeve.

It's four a.m., mum said, and Lou still isn't home.

Maybe he decided to spend the night somewhere else. He was pretty pissed off at you I recall.

Did he say that?

No. Yes. I mean, I heard the two of you fighting before you left.

So where do you think he went?

Maybe he's sleeping over at a friend's.

He doesn't have any friends, mum said.

Pop was about to suggest that Lou had found one, but mum looked pretty abject and Pop was afraid to push her over the edge by suggesting that Lou may have hooked up with some floozy. Maybe he's sleeping it off in an alley someplace, Pop said.

Maybe we should go out and look for him?

Where?

You know, around the neighborhood. Will you drive me?

No.

Why not?

Because I think you're making a capital case of it. He'll come home when he wants to. In the meantime, you and I should get some sleep.

But mum didn't sleep. She went back to the kitchen and smoked cigarettes till dawn. The smoke haze cat arching its back against the ceiling gave birth to a litter of fog kittens; they loped into the living room and throughout the house leaving airy smoke paw prints everywhere they went.

In the morning, mum asked Pop if she should report Lou missing.

Premature, he said.

In the afternoon, she asked Pop if she should report Lou missing.

He's been gone less than 24 hours, Pop said.

That evening, she asked again what Pop thought she should do.

I don't think you should do anything, Pop said.

Mum sat down in Lou's chair and opened a fresh pack of cigarettes, her third that day by Pop's count. What's that? she asked, pointing to a spot on the carpet.

Where? Pop asked.

Right there, mum said, pointing.

It's probably Jack and coke, Pop said. Lou may have spilled some while he was sitting there drinking.

No, it doesn't look like coca cola, mum said. It looks more like blood or something. Mum got up from her chair and was about to bend down to sniff the spot on the carpet when Pop stopped her. Just sit yourself back down, mum, he said. I'll get a scrub brush and clean it up. Stay, he ordered over his shoulder as he left the room.

Mum did as she was told and sat back down in the recliner while Pop went to get a brush and a wash rag. He sat down on the carpet, causing his knee to crackle, and began to diligently scrub the spot where Evelyn had been pointing.

You did see him? mum said to the top of his head.

I'm sorry, mum, Pop said, looking up at her. What did you say?

I said you saw Lou last night?

Mum, we've been all through that.

You said he was sitting in his recliner drinking jack and coke.

Yeah, Pop said, I guess he was. For a little bit after you went out.

Did he say anything?

Just that he was pissed off at you, that's all.

Did he say anything else, you know, did he give any clue as to where he might be going?

Well, he didn't tell me he was going anywhere. But, hey, you know, he likes to go to Florida this time of year.

He'd have told me if he was going to Florida.

You and he weren't speaking to each other, were you?

No, mum said glumly. She lit another cigarette, took a drag or two from it, and stubbed it out. He wouldn't have just walked out and gone to Florida without taking anything, she declared. You know, like his clothes, and all.

No, he probably wouldn't, Pop agreed.

Mum got up and went into the master bedroom. Pop could hear her opening cabinets and looking in drawers. She emerged from the bedroom a few minutes later looking quite distraught.

His clothes are still here, she declared.

Sure?

Sure.

Pop got up and went into the master bedroom. He opened a couple of cabinet drawers and slammed them shut.

I didn't see that green shirt in there, the one he really likes, Pop said. Some of his polos are missing, too, and a couple of plaid shorts.

He'd have taken more than that.

Maybe he likes to travel light.

Did he take his suitcase? Mum asked.

I'll go down into the basement and look, Pop volunteered.

Pop emerged a few minutes later, shaking his head. It's gone, he said.

Sure?

I'm sure.

Evelyn wanted to call Lou's brother in Florida to see if Lou was there, but Pop reminded her that Lou's brother had died a few years ago. Neither of them could recall where Lou liked to stay. Evelyn thought that she needed to call somebody, but she didn't know who to call. And that was where she left it, in a state of indecision that lasted over the course of several days.

Lou became little more than a lingering memory over the next few days as Evelyn turned to the bottle for companionship. She had never needed men as much as she needed booze. Pop got a call from the Lyceum a couple of times to come and get her because she was obnoxiously drunk. Some drunks are fun to be with, the liquor lighting them up like stars. Others are fun to be around because they can be quite entertaining in their hot mess, train wreck ways. In the entertainment category, Pop was partial to the women who were transformed by alcohol into super sluts (except when the super slut was his mother), but he didn't have much patience for the alcohol-fueled man whores who were always chatting up the super sluts he wanted to bed down. Pop also wasn't partial to the drama queens or Nancy Boys who would get all sentimental and emotional whenever they got drunk. As bad as these types were, at least they weren't mean. Evelyn was a mean drunk.

Sure you didn't do somethin' to Lou? she asked one night after Pop picked her up at the Lyceum.

No, mum, he said.

Sure?

Sure.

I don't fuckin' believe you.

Okay, fine. Believe what you want.

No, you fuckin' did something, mum said in that gravely Evelyn voice of hers. I know you fuckin' did somethin'.

Okay, fine. What do you think I did?

I don't know, she said.

Pop made the right turn from Fernleaf onto Salisbury and put some pedal to the metal.

Slow down, Evelyn growled. I don't need you to kill me, too.

Yeah, that's what I did, Pop said, in a peeved tone of voice. I put a stake in Lou's heart, and left him in his coffin in the basement. Or maybe I hacked him to pieces and froze his organs so you'd have some liver to eat with your onions.

No one likes a smart shit, mum replied. I know you done somethin', she said, as Pop pulled into their driveway. I don't know what, but I know you done somethin',

A few days later, Lou was back on the menu as Issue Du Jour. Mum had been to the UPS Store where Lou rented a mail box. The clerk there asked mum if Lou was okay. It seems he hadn't been around to pick up his mail and his box was getting full. This got mum to thinking about Lou's social security and pension checks, which were direct deposited to his banking account. Lou had an account in his own name; his finances, in fact, were so separate from Evelyn's that she didn't know his account number. Pop and Evelyn had scoured the house looking for Lou's checkbook, but they couldn't find it – evidence, Pop said, that Lou had walked out on her.

Mum wasn't willing to accept that. She didn't think he would go anywhere without cash on hand, and she didn't know if he had cash because she didn't know if he was taking money out of his account, and his bank wouldn't tell her. I'm his wife, she told the teller. Your name isn't on the account, he said. I'm his wife, she told the assistant bank manager. Your name isn't on the account, he said. I'm his wife, she told the manager. Mam, he said, I can't even confirm that Mr. Wisniewski even so much as has an account with this branch.

Mum decided to see a lawyer. And, of course, being mum, she didn't see a good one, choosing instead to consult with one of her bar buddies, some neighborhood shyster who spend more time in the saloon than in his office, and even less time in court. Quite unsurprisingly, mum's lawyer buddy didn't know how Evelyn could get into Lou's account, not until or unless he was declared dead, but he suggested that mum might want to contact the Social Security Administration to enlist its help in finding him. He also suggested that it was time, well past time actually, to report Lou missing to the police.

Mum did as she was told. She went to SSA, but all the agency did was charge her $25 to send a letter to Lou asking him to contact her. And since the only address Social Security had for Lou was his P.O. Box, the letter went there, and eventually got returned to SSA, which refused to refund the $25 dollars when mum asked for it back.

Mum also reported Lou missing. When Pop refused to drive her, she walked all the way to the Zone 3 station, which was two or three miles away from where they lived. She filed a report, and talked to an officer there. He said they would get Lou's dental records and put his info into a national tracking system once he had been missing for more than a month.

Can't you do anything before then? Evelyn wanted to know.

Yeah, yeah, yeah, the officer told her. We'll be working on it.

Why do you need his dental records? she asked.

Well, you know, the officer told her. In the event there's been foul play. The officer assured her that wasn't likely. Most missing persons get found when they want to be found, he said.

A month and a half later, Lou's car was found in the parking lot of the Pittsburgh International Airport.

See, mum, Pop said. I was right. He probably went to Florida like I said.

Mum said she was inclined to believe that, but she didn't understand why Lou hadn't called her, or at least given the UPS Store a forwarding address.

Getting the car back was a hassle. The Allegheny County police had it towed from the airport to a garage, but when mum went to claim it, the garage people wouldn't give it to her. Even though mum and Lou were married, the car was registered in his name. Moreover, the garage wanted to charge mum for towing and storage. Plus, the airport parking authority wanted paid for the time Lou's car had sat in the airport parking lot. All told, the charges were close to $1,500.00. Lou may have had money in the bank, but Evelyn didn't. Because her license was suspended, she couldn't drive the vehicle anyway, so she threw up her hands and decided to let the garage sell the car. (They said the law authorized them to do this, even without Lou signing over title to the car. There was a statute that dealt with it, they said). That way, the amount she owed would be less, although the garage said they would still have to come after her for it.

Later, Evelyn had second thoughts about letting them sell the car. Fingerprints, she said. Didn't anyone check for fingerprints?

Why, Pop asked. I mean, no one had any reason to suspect that he had been abducted.

Just in case, Evelyn said. Just in case that happened.

Well, you know, Pop told her, if Lou had been taken at gunpoint somewhere, his assailant probably wiped the car clean of prints.

You think so? Mum said.

Yeah, I think so.

So, mum let the garage sell the car, and that was that. The garage came after her for more money, and she never paid it, and the account went into collections, and they got dunning calls from time to time. And, after a while, Lou became a forbidden topic of conversation for Pop and Evelyn. Christmas passed, as did the winter months, but Lou never returned from Florida or wherever he had gone, and they thought about him less and less. Occasionally, mum would mumble something about that rotten lousy bastard that she married or she would shout out Lou's name in her sleep, and every once in a while she would look at Pop through her cold green eyes and say, I know you did somethin' to him. I know you did. But mum could never prove anything and no one else seemed to care.

Perry & Dick

In America, people go missing all the time. Some of them are run-away teenagers who can't stand their parents or just feel enclosed by their lives and think there's something better out there someplace else. In the next city, across the state line, somewhere further down the highway. Some are goateed young men with alcohol or drug addictions. Some are clean-shaven adults with credit or gambling problems. Some are young women with stardust in their eyes and rhythm in their feet. Some dream of romantic far-away places. Some just want to escape. Some have wanderlust in their souls. Some are middle-aged people who wonder what their lives might have been like if had followed the beat of a different drummer or just taken the other path, the less trodden one, at the proverbial fork in the road. Some are elderly men and women who just go wandering off, like the household cat or dog after someone leaves the back door open or fails to shut the front gate. Some, quite a few actually, are children. Some are white, some are black, some are Latino or Hispanic. People who keep statistics on these things say that about 2,300 people are reported missing in America every day, or close to a million people a year. Pop wondered where all the missing people went.

He had a theory. It didn't explain all of them, but it explained some of them. The theory, quite simply, was that they had been abducted, not by psychopaths lurking behind masks of sanity, nor by cold-blooded necrophiles, killer clowns or cannibalistic drifters, either. No, quite simply, they had been abducted by agents of their own government.

Pop had learned about it from Glenn Beck. Pop was watching Beck being interviewed by Brian Kilmeade on Fox and Friends one morning. They were talking about a secret letter from Obama to Putin offering to pull the plug on a defense missile system for the Czech Republic if Russia helped prevent Iran from acquiring nuclear weapons. Kilmeade was saying that the Czechs had been sold out. Well, they understand freedom, Glenn Beck said, which is more than you can say for us. We are a country that is headed toward socialism, totalitarianism, beyond your wildest imagination. I have to tell you, Glenn Beck said, I'm doing a story tonight that I wanted to debunk these FEMA camps. You know about them? I wanted to debunk them. Well, we've now for several days done research on them. I can't debunk them.

Pop nearly spit out his morning apple juice when he heard that. For years, ever since he read about REX 84 and HSPD 20 and 51, he had suspected that ZOG was building concentration camps. It was all being done under the guise of disaster relief, like those mobile trailers FEMA bought for Hurricane Katrina victims. But the camps weren't being built to shelter those whose homes were lost as a result of a hurricane or flood or some such other natural disaster – no, sir, they were intended as relocation camps for people the government found dangerous, god-fearing, gun-toting red meat eating Americans like Pop himself (except for the god-fearing part). Pop had read about it on the internet. Now, here was Glenn Beck telling him that it was true.

It is our government, Beck continued. If you trust our government, it's fine. If you have any kind of fear that we may be headed toward a totalitarian state, look out, buckle up. There is something going on in our country that is – ain't good.

Pop didn't need Glenn Beck to tell him that the country was going to hell. Between bailouts to investment banking firms like Goldman Sachs and a federal deficit that was more than $6 trillion, it was clear where the economy was headed, and the direction was south. Pop fully expected that B.O. would take America over the cliff, spending the country into a Second Great Depression, or something even worse. So, Beck's assessment that there was something going on in the country that wasn't good was hardly news. But Beck confirmed Pop's fear that once chaos came, the ZOG would react by rounding up patriots and putting them in camps. And the fact that Beck walked back his statement that he couldn't debunk the FEMA camps within twenty-four hours of making it only confirmed Pop's gut feeling that the camps were real. Someone got to him, Pop told KG. Someone told him to shut up about the camps.

Through the internet, Pop had learned that the ultra-liberal Alcee Hastings had introduced a bill – H.R. 645 – that directed the Secretary of Homeland Security to establish national emergency centers on military installations. Pop knew there used to be a top secret installation on South Mountain near Blue Ridge Summit on the Maryland-Pennsylvania line – he had driven there once on his way to a WNist rally at Antietam, and had gotten lost and turned onto a secluded mountain road, only to be stopped at a gate by a couple of uniformed men who told him he couldn't go any further. Fort Ritchie, as it was called, was where the government trained some 10,000 emigrants, mostly German-Jews and Austrians, in methods of interrogation, investigation, and psy-ops and then air-dropped them behind the front lines during World War II in an attempt to establish a fifth column within Nazi Germany. The so-called "Ritchie Boys" were supposed to have been instrumental in defeating Hitler. The site continued to be a Military Intelligence Training Center after the war until being "closed" in 1998, quite a few years before Pop got lost there and got asked to leave. He was sure that something was still going on at Fort Ritchie – hell, there has been a psy-ops camp near Gettysburg, too -- and he had read on Stormtroop and other sites on the internet that the government was building relocation camps at the former federal prison camp in Allenwood and at Indiantown Gap, a military reservation that had been used to house POWs during WW II.

What to do? What to do? What to do? Pop asked KG. The answer was clear: get ready for the inevitable. Make like a Boy Scout, and be prepared.

Pop made like a Boy Scout. He bought cases of bottled water and stacked them in the basement. He bought dehydrated food and freeze-dried storable food from internet websites that specialized in supplying food that would keep for a long time, food you could use in any type of emergency. (He steered away from Meals, Ready to Eat, or MREs, because he didn't think they were a good value.) He bought candles. He purchased box matches, batteries, and toilet paper in 40-roll cartons. He bought camping gear, propane, and a propane camping stove. If he had more money, he would have bought a generator.

Instead, he maxed out his credit card on ammo, a new .357 and body armor. The .357 rounded out the arsenal he had been building over the years, the shining centerpiece of which was the AK-47 he had bought on First Wednesday, as he called it, the day after Obama was elected. Pop especially liked the AK because it was one of those weapons liberals get all steamed up about, referred to it as an "assault weapon," and totally missing the fact that it was just semi-automatic, and not a fully automatic rifle like liberals, in their stark ignorance, thought it was. (Real automatic weapons and real automatic military rifles have been heavily regulated since 1934 and banned from new manufacture since 1986, which just goes to show that libs don't know what they're talking about.)

Like the AK, Pop got the .357 at a local gun shop with a camouflage-colored storefront, bars in the windows and stone perimeter barriers that made it as secure as a government building. (Pop had actually purchased the AK over the internet, but had it delivered, for a fee, to the shop owner, a federally licensed gun dealer, as required by federal law). The .357 was a Smith & Wesson 686, blued (He had wanted a Colt Python, which was becoming more of a collector's piece, but got the 686 instead.) The vest was Level II German Kevlar, more than good enough to stop a shot from a cop's .40 caliber handgun or Pop's own 9mm Glock. Pop modeled the vest for KG and had his friend take a couple of shots of him in it while he was holding his AK. Pop scanned the photos into his computer and uploaded them to a Stormtroop forum under the caption, Don't fuck with me.

Pop figured you could never be too prepared. He took to sleeping with the .357 under his pillow and some extra ammo under the bed. He had nightmares that someone would come to get him while he slept. Insomnia plagued him. He started getting up in the middle of the night and performing endless searches on the internet, sometimes googling the FEMA camps, sometimes googling Keilah, once even googling Kathy Cohen, but mostly just looking for advice on how to get by in a world gone mad. Survivalist sites had a special appeal to him. He spent hours browsing natural disasters, sudden pandemics, visions of apocalypse. He liked to read about guns. He second-guessed his purchases. He wondered if he should have held out for the Colt. He wondered if he should have bought a Level III vest, if it would have been worth the extra weight. He wondered if he should have opted for military grade armor, like the kind Larry Phillips and Emil Matasareanu wore in the North Hollywood shootout when they kept the whole damn LAPD at bay until Phillips popped himself in the head and someone shot Matasareanu in the legs and feet, causing him to bleed out. (Pop had seen a documentary about the shootout on TV.)

One especially agitated night, Pop searched for information on the German POWs who were housed at Fort Ritchie during World War II. He read that they were forced to perform day labor on nearby farms and that they were taunted by black soldiers who shouted "Heil Hitler! Heil Hitler" at them through the fence. He felt sympathy for the POWs, even though they were on the wrong side. Empathy relaxed him and he fell asleep at the computer, waking up in a heart-pounding panic, fully convinced that someone, a neighborhood gang perhaps, was trying to break in. He got dressed and took his AK-47 outside and walked the perimeter of the house and yard. He heard a dog barking. He heard an animal cry. He saw shadows dart and weave, but he didn't see anyone, not a person, nothing remotely human, just leafy bushes and tree branches swaying in the wind, creating chiaroscuro effects on the ground. Pop smoked a cigarette to calm himself. He shouldered the AK and went back inside, but thoughts of an intruder or intruders still haunted him. In the non-rem state that passed for his sleep, he thought he heard someone digging a tunnel from the yard into the house. The noise startled him, and in his terror, he thought he saw black faces at a window shouting "Heil Hitler! Heil Hitler" at him through the windowpanes.

Pop's neighborhood was racially mixed. There once had been demarcation lines that separated the black areas from the white, but then the projects closed and the lines got blurred as low-income housing got decentralized and Section 8 apartments started springing up everywhere. (Hell, the house next door that the crack addicts lived in was Section 8.) Pop didn't like it. The new urban planning was bringing the neighborhood down, chasing out people with jobs and leaving the unemployed crack heads like his neighbor and the unemployed alkies like his mother and the unemployed mush heads like himself. (What's my addiction? Pop wondered. You're addicted to love, his good angel said. You're addicted to hate, his bad angel replied. He had to agree with the shoulder angel on his left, the little cloven-hoofed guy – like most Americans, he was boiling with anger, buttons already pushed, rage flowing out of him like untreated effluvium. Hate was what he had in common with the other people on his block, in his town, his state, his country, his world.)

For an American like Pop, the most dominant emotion was hate's cousin --revenge. Not love, not friendship, not sexual desire. (Supposedly, libertine Americans still put a fig leaf on the penis – the one thing you can't see on television; jealousy was their aphrodisiac, not ginko biloba, cialis or cantharidin.) Even greed and envy lagged far behind. Americans perceived just about anything as a slight and talked in terms of getting even and payback. Their middle fingers were always raised. Revenge fantasies dotted their collective consciousness and revenge themes underlay their music and their movies. The soundtrack in their heads was playing "I'm Gonna Get Me a Gun" and "F.U.R.B. (Fuck U Right Back)" and Blue Oyster Cult's "Power Underneath Despair." The loop in their heads was screening Carrie and Death Wish and Kill Bill. Americans were channeling their inner Max Rockatanskys, John Creasys and David Sumners. They were too busy plotting revenge to read, but if they had their heads in a book it would have been Moby Dick ("to the last I grapple with thee; from hell's heart I stab at thee; for hate's sake I spit my last breath at thee.") There's a reason why the rich old Americans who prefer theatres to movie houses flock to see Hamlet instead of King Lear.

Pop wanted to get even with the crack heads next door. Crack Daddy (Pop's name for the man of the house) and his teenage kiddies were always leaving paraphernalia in mum's yard – bits of copper brillo pad, sections of rifle cleaning rod, and pieces of car deodorizer, the kind that comes in long, glass-tube like bottles and got used as crack pipes (the brillo was used as a screen to hold and burn the crack and the cleaning rod served to push the brillo from one end of the "pipe" to another, tightening up the screen and pushing the resins back, making for a good crack-resin hit.) Pop found McDonald's quarter-pound hamburger wrappers and fries boxes on his side of the fence, too. One day, Pop saw Crack Daddy walking his dog; the dog, a Rottweiler, squatted and took a dump on the sidewalk directly in front of Pop's house. When the dog was done, the neighbor started to walk away. Hey, man, Pop said, coming down the front steps, aren't you going to clean up after your animal? The Rottweiler looked up at Pop, showing him his teeth. The man put some slack in the leash. If it bothers you, he said, why don't you clean it up? Cause he's your dog and he just took a dump in my yard. That ain't your yard, the man said. It's the sidewalk. You don't own the sidewalk. The city does. Look man, that ain't the point, Pop said. The point is I have to walk there. But the man was already showing Pop his back, acting like he didn't hear, or, more than likely, didn't care. The dog looked back and yipped at Pop as they left.

Pop thought about jumping over the fence once night and taking a dump on the crack head's front porch, his way of saying "call." But everyone in the house stayed up all night and he thought the yippy Rottweiler would bark. Pop fantasized about mailing a parcel of shit to the neighbors, or putting a shit sandwich in one of those McDonalds wrappers he found all over his yard. Then he hit upon a plan that was much more viable: He would get his own dog and let him crap on the neighbor's sidewalk, his front stoop and porch.

The plan in action, in execution, as it were, was even better than the plan on the drawing board. Instead of one dog, Pop got two. They were American pit bull pups, both male. One of them was brown with a white stripe down the middle of its brick-like head; the other was white with a black ring around one of its eyes that reminded Pop of Petey, the dog in The Little Rascals, sans the circled eye that make-up artist Max Factor had painted on, of course. (Pop read somewhere that Pete the Pup was poisoned by someone who fed him meat with glass in it, and that after he died he was buried with Alfalfa, who was shot to death at the age of 31.) Each of Pop's pups had a well-muscled neck that ran into a deep, well-sprung chest and stocky, gun-barrel body that ended in a tail tapered to a point. Each pup's teeth formed a scissor's bite. Chew on that, Pop wanted to say to his neighbor when he brought the dogs home from the Animal Rescue League where he had found them and probably saved them from being euthanized (although, to be sure, they got put down after Pop committed the crime that landed him on Death Row.)

Pop wasn't sure what to call them, but he instantly ruled out all the pair names, like Ricky and Lucy or Bonnie and Clyde, that included a woman's given name. (He didn't want anyone to think one of his pups was gay.) That still left him with an abundance of choices.

He thought about Judge and Jury, Trouble and Mischief, Thunder and Bolt, Ruff and Tumble, Tango and Cash, Starsky and Hutch, and even Stud and Muffin (although Muffin was definitely a female name). He thought about gangster names like Mad Dog and Machine Gun, Bugsy and Scarface, Torio and Capone. He thought about gunslinger names like Butch and Sundance. He toyed with Holmes and Watson, and Holmes and Moriarty. Trying to find the appropriate note of savagery, he entertained calling them Skull and Bones, Tool and Die, Uday and Qusay, Hiroshima and Nagasaki. Finally, he settled upon Perry and Dick, after Perry Smith and Richard Hickok, the two killers Lou Wisniewski had told him about. He thought it was a fitting tribute to his stepfather, laced with just the right amount of irony.

Mum was none too pleased about the dogs. I got them for you, Pop said. As a present. Present my ass, mum said. They'll keep us safe, Pop said. Who'll keep us safe from them, Evelyn retorted. Seriously, mum, Pop said. They'll give the crack heads next door something to think about, and they'll let us know if someone's trying to break in. Plus pit bulls can be very friendly – don't believe what you read – and you may like having them just for the companionship, you know what I mean? Look, Evelyn said, arms crossed in front of her. Don't give me this man's best friend your best friend bullshit. A woman's best friend ain't a dog, it's diamonds and chocolate, and if you wanted to give me a real present that's what you would have got me. So cut the crap. They're your dogs. Just make sure you feed 'em and walk 'em and train 'em.

And so he did. Pop got the pups house-broken in about a week. He took the pups out for a walk bright and early every morning – too early to make much of an impression on the neighbors who didn't rise much before noon. When he was house-breaking them, Pop took the pups outside every few hours during the day. The trick was to give the pups a treat when they pottied. Pop also took their water bowl up a few hours before going to bed. Even so, one of the pups – Perry – often woke Pop up during the night with his whining, a sign that he needed to pee. Pop would dress and take the dog out to do his business when that happened.

In the evening, Pop liked to walk Perry and Dick past the neighbor's house. He got in the habit of stopping right outside the front stoop, and after a while both pups got the hint and used it as a place to pee. Neither one of the dogs liked to poop there though, preferring a grassy spot in the woods behind Pop's house. Still, Pop would give the pups a treat every time they took a whiz in front of the crack head's house.

Once, not long after Pop got the dogs, Crack Daddy was sitting on the front steps when Pop took Perry and Dick out for their evening walk. Puppy wanna make poopie? Pop said, as he paused with the dogs near the front stoop. Pop could feel Crack Daddy's eyes boring into him like an awl through leather. Don't be having your dogs shitting on my sidewalk, the crack addict said. Oh, it's your sidewalk here but mine belongs to the City, Pop told him. They'll shit where they want to shit, he said. Crack Daddy got up off of his haunches then and started to stride down the steps. Dick's ears perked up as the man approached, and the dog began to growl. Perry joined in seconds later, adding harmony to Dick's melody, although the sounds they were producing were best described as cacophony. Crack Daddy looked at the dogs, thought better of whatever it was he was thinking, and turned and went inside his house. Good, boy, Perry, Pop said, handing the dog a treat. Good, dog, Dick, he said, giving one to the other puppy. Neither of the dogs had pooped or pissed, but Pop figured they were entitled to treats on the strength of their performance alone.

Perry and Dick were partial to chew treats. They were especially partial to Buffalo Stix made by some company called Canine Caviar. The Stix were made of dried pizzle from free-range, grass-fed buffalo. The pizzle came from the buffalo's penis. To make it, the animal's penis was removed and cleaned and hung vertically to allow the fluids to run out. Then the pizzle was stretched and twisted and dried and smoked and cut into six- to twelve-inches pieces. Pop thought it was funny that Dick literally liked eating dick. The only problem with giving it to him was that Buffalo Stix cost more than cow pizzle, even pizzle that came from free-ranging bulls. So Pop alternated the Buffalo Stix with bully sticks. The other problem was that Perry tended to like braided sticks while Dick preferred the straight ones. Different strokes for different folks, Pop chuckled as he gave the treats to his dogs.

He had one more encounter with Crack Daddy after that, but the dogs weren't with him at the time. Pop had found some more McDonalds wrappers and fries boxes on his side of the fence, lying next to a couple of broken chopsticks, which, Pop figured, the crack heads had used as a substitute for a cleaning rod while they were making their fix. He picked the trash up, carried it next door, and set it down on the neighbor's porch. As he did, he saw Crack Daddy looking out at him through the screen door. What the fuck you think yo doin'? Crack Daddy said through the screen. What the fuck you think yo' doin'? Pop replied. Our yard's not your litter box. So keep your trash and your crack makin's over here where they belong. Yeah? The neighbor said, as he opened the screen door. As the door swung open, Pop caught a glimpse of his own reflection in the mirror of his mind. You talkin' to me? the reflection said. You talkin' to me?

Yeah, Pop said, as the man came out on the porch and stood toe to toe with him. Pop casually swept back his unbuttoned shirt to reveal the Bersa Thunder in his waist band. Don't fuck with me, Pop said, raising a finger and pointing it at the man. Don't ever fuck with me again, Pop said. Ever. Understand? But the man didn't say anything. He looked at the Bersa, calculated that he didn't want to risk it, and quietly stepped back inside the doorway, closing the screen behind him before shutting the front door. Pop stood triumphantly on the porch for a moment. He heard someone suppress a cough and thought he saw a pair of eyes, a child's perhaps, looking out at him through the window blinds. Boo! Pop said, as he thrust his face against the window glass. The blinds snapped shut with a twang. Someone whispered ("Is he still there?"). A moment passed. Pop thought he heard a clicking sound, like someone pulling the slide of a gun. Then nothing. He felt like the whole house was holding its breath. Pop didn't know how long he waited on the porch for the walls, the windows, the screen door to exhale, for someone to come out, for something else to happen (he half-expected Crack Daddy, or one of his children, to step out holding a semiautomatic weapon in his hands), but no one appeared, and the neighborhood finally took a breath. When it was clear that nothing more was going to happen, Pop spat disdainfully on the ground. Fucking niggers, he said, out loud, before going back to his house to feed his dogs.

***

The sound of a flapping window shade. Memories flickering like film through a projector. Fireflies in a glass jar. Goldfish in a bowl. I am in a cell, not this one, another one, a cell in the county jail where I was housed before they brought me to SCI-Garrow. I was on suicide watch, having refused psychotropic meds, and there was a surveillance camera pointed at me. I was naked. Stark naked. They had not only taken my belt and shoe laces, they had also taken my shoes, my clothes and my underwear. The camera blinked at me, like an eye, a beady red eye. I disabled it, smashing the lens with my fist. And then the officers came to take me to the mental health unit. The lead one had a Lexan gladiator body shield and used it to pin me to the cot in the cell. I felt like I was being put under a microscope. Look, see, this is the maggot's head, note the tiny, teeth-like fangs extending from its mouth. See, here, the parasitic nematodes inside the insect belly, look, there, at its spiny penis. Kneeling on his shield, the officer pressed my head and chest against the cot, squishing me like a bug. The other COs in the room leered at me, making obscene comments about my body, my genitals, and I cursed them, wishing them all dead. One of them held a camera and recorded the incident, which was played back at my trial as proof I lacked remorse.

***

Pop's encounter with the neighbor was nothing like the one he had later with his mum. She was sick and tired of his bullshit. (I'm sick and tired of yours, too, he thought.) She was tired of him sitting around on his ass all the time doing nothing. (Maybe you'd be more energized, he thought, if you got up off your precious ass every once in a while, too.) She was sick of his behavior, like the rudeness he displayed to the neighbors or the attitude he was giving here right now. (I'm overcome with consternation about your ongoing passivity in the face of un-neighborly aggression, Pop wanted to tell her, and if you think this is attitude, just wait.) She was tired of him and his fucking dogs. (I guess that makes you dog-tired, Pop chuckled to himself, but a conversation with mum wasn't any laughing matter. Hell, it wasn't even a conversation, just a nonstop monologue with an infinitely recycling loop of points and issues and admonitions and reminders.)

The main point, the big issue, the real deal, the one behind her constant admonitions and reminders, came down to one thing. One word. Money. Evelyn didn't have any. She missed all the free drinks she got when Lou was her constant companion, buying the rounds, and she hadn't yet figured out a way to get at his social security and pension checks. Evelyn was cash-strapped, and she hadn't found another alkie pal to leech onto.

Money was beginning to be a problem for Pop, too. His creditors called on almost a daily basis. They wanted to know when he would pay, and when he said he couldn't pay, they threatened to put his accounts into collection or to take him to court. It reached the point where he was afraid to answer the phone, which rang virtually off the hook, at all times of day, between the hours of 8 a.m. and 9 p.m., of course, as proscribed by the Fair Debt Collection Practices Act.

There were the dunning letters, too. Pop accumulated quite a big stack of them. They all wanted the same thing. Money. Money. Money.

Pop thought about getting a job, but his damn knee still wasn't right and he knew he couldn't do the same kind of work he had done in Palm Glades or Butler or Ridgeway. Hell, he couldn't even work as a stock boy like he had done for Mr. Savage because he couldn't physically do the job. Mentally, he had hit such a low point that he thought he could do the bowing and the scraping, but he couldn't do the lifting, the standing, and the kneeling (especially the kneeling, which was, perhaps, the most important part of any job available to him anywhere in America, metaphorically speaking).

Mum didn't care about his effin' knee. She didn't care about all his excuses. The only thing she wanted to know was how long it was going to be until he became a man and stood up on his own hind legs and started making a contribution to the household. Pop knew where she was going with this, and he promised himself he wasn't going to let Evelyn push his buttons anymore.

He waited until she went to the bathroom, or got up to make herself another drink, and went into her purse and took a couple of bills. Then he called KG and asked him if he wanted to meet at the bar and toss a couple back for old time's sake.

They drank until two in the morning, mostly on KG's dime, and got themselves crocked (well, Pop did, KG switching to soda after a while, and making excuses for doing so – he had to work in the morning, he said). So when the bar closed, KG went home and didn't invite Pop back with him, and they didn't have the all-night bull session Pop had been looking forward to and inwardly hoped they'd have. Fortunately, Evelyn wasn't up when Pop got back to his house and he slipped into his room without another confrontation. Unfortunately, he was so keyed up he couldn't sleep. He thought about watching TV, but was afraid the noise might wake Evelyn up and he didn't want to be reamed out by her again that evening. So he turned the computer on and got on the internet and went on the Raw Meaty Bones website and read about feeding his puppies a natural diet of chicken, rabbit and turkey carcasses, fish heads and offal. After a while, he checked out the day's news, following a Fox News link to a story about some guy who went berserk in Binghamton, New York, opening fire at an immigration center and killing fourteen people at a citizenship class. The man, who turned out to be some gook who emigrated from Vietnam, had recently been laid off from his job and was living on unemployment benefits before something snapped inside and he took his revenge. Pop didn't like gooks but he could understand how someone could be pushed to the edge and reach a point where he just couldn't stand things anymore.

Pop couldn't stand things anymore. He couldn't stand his mother. He couldn't stand his neighbors. He couldn't stand his fucking life. If his life were a film, it would record all the sovereign accidents that had made him what he was, or unmade him, as it were, the people, like Mr. Savage, who had shit on him, missing his Christian moment, or, in Mr. Savage's case, the moment of performing a mitzvoth, a quotidian act of kindness to a stranger, places, like Palm Glades or Pittsburgh or Butler or Ridgeway, which reinforced his aloneness rather than loaning him a sense of community, of belongingness, or events, like Keilah leaving him or Kathy Cohen blaming him or his grandfather dying or his grandmother going bonkers or just being born to a bitch like Evelyn, you pick one, you name it, you tell him how he could have summoned up the will to transcend the immutable, impersonal and immanent forces that had shaped him and made him what he was, is, and forever will be. All Pop could tell you was that he was sick of the projection on the screen, the repeating reel, the un-reel of his life, and he wanted to get past the climax of his story, to the falling action, to the end, past the list of characters, the credits and the blames, all the way to the blank empty screen, where maybe he could start all over again and write his name in a different script, or just rejoice in the fact that it was over.

Around five, the alcohol and the freneticism of his thoughts started to exhaust him, to tug his eyelids down toward the floor, to the nadir where his soul was, and he fell asleep. Somewhere outside of himself, in a place beyond dreams and nightmares, he felt something nip at his feet and heard something whimpering, a dog perhaps, or the child he couldn't ever remember having been.

<u>Me</u>

Spread your cheeks, one of the COs said, after returning me to my cell from the shower. I was waiting for him to tell me it was all right to get dressed, when he put a hand on the small of my back and leaned in toward me. I felt his fetid breath on my neck. Hey, he sneered, you think you've got it rough on Death Row, don't you buddy? You know, Pop, he expectorated, his spit spray landing on my right shoulder, if you were in general one of the cons there would have popped your cherry a long time ago. One of the other COs chuckled at his little word play on my name. I tried to rise from the bent over position I was in when the CO who was strip searching me said, whoa, hang on. We're not finished here, buddy, he said. I wanted to ask him if he liked the view up my ass, but didn't, not wanting to risk any reprisals from the group of COs, four of them, who were in my cell. Yes sir, mister, the CO who was strip searching me said, that's a fact. They'd have busted your cherry long ago. In fact, you wouldn't have been safe here either under the old administration. He pushed down on my back when he said this, and I felt my sphincter tighten and I braced myself for something really bad, fully expecting him to

186

thrust a baton up my asshole. Instead, he told me to get dressed. Consider yourself lucky, mister, he said. You're probably going to die a virgin.

After they left, I sat down on my cot and reached for my tablet. I wanted to encode the experience, write it down. As I picked up the tablet, I noticed that it was folded open to a page where someone had scrawled, "This is shit. You are shit, too." My first instinct was to interpret the words as jailhouse literary criticism of my writing, rather than a literalism, but then I saw the turd sitting in my crate, on top of my white underwear. Goddamn it, I said out loud. Goddamn it.

I put down the tablet and got a tissue and picked up the turd and flushed it down the toilet. Then I took my underwear, both pairs of them, and shoved them into the bowl, too. Of course, they didn't flush. I watched the water fill the bowl and began to trickle over the sides of the toilet, onto the floor of my cell.

I sat back down on my cot and watched the water pool on the floor. After a while, the CO's came. They handcuffed me and moved me to another cell in the RHU while they cleaned up mine. This one had a toilet/sink and a bunk with a bare mattress. Nothing else. The COs had me stand facing the wall. Don't move! Don't touch the wall! one of them screamed, and, for a moment, I thought I was back in the Corps again. I was instructed to place my left hand on the top of my head after they removed the left handcuff, and to keep it there while they removed the right. I was told to put my right hand on the top of my head and to keep it there with the other one after they removed the remaining handcuff. Then, I got strip-searched again, the COs pushing and tugging my body with their nightsticks. Before they were through, one of them leaned in and shouted full volume in my ear that if I fucked with the toilet again, he would stick my head in the bowl and flush it into the Monongahela River or wherever the pipes led.

After I was strip searched they took my prison uniform away and gave me another one, but didn't give me any socks or underwear or slippers. I wasn't given any sheets for the mattress or a blanket. NO TP or soap, either. They locked me in the new cell, which felt strange and unfamiliar and stank of the other inmates who had resided in it before. After they locked me in, they left.

It was cold in the cell and, without a blanket, I shivered all night. I had felt some momentary euphoria when I was taken from my cell, but that quickly vanished and was replaced by the cold, hard depressing truth that I was being punished for what I had done and that the punishment wouldn't end until the lesson had sunk in. That night, I dreamed I was an angel floating over America. From the air, from my vantage point, half of the country was in darkness while the other half was bathed in light. The light was brightest on the northeastern seaboard, where America's most luminous cities are, but there was also some light streaming out of the darkness, from those places in Kansas or Montana or wherever the smaller cities were; the intense pinpricks of illumination reminded me of shooting stars or the pattern a Roman candle makes when it explodes. I thought about the tequila salt on Dick Nixon's skin. I imagined constellations, burning sun shapes inside an amoeba-like splash or spray, and when I awoke, the light on the ceiling of the cell was staring back at me like a large and naked eye.

The next day, one of the COs shoved a roll of toilet paper and a small bar of soap through the pie hole in the cell door. Later, I was given a handle-less toothbrush and a small tube of toothpaste. The COs also fed me, but they didn't take me back to my cell and they didn't let me out to exercise or to shower.

After a few days of this, I got really stir crazy, crazier than I had ever been since I was incarcerated. I woke up one night to discover that the nails of my hands were broken and the walls of the cell were streaked with blood, the result, apparently, of my attempts to scratch and claw my way out.

That little episode earned me a trip to the psychiatric observation unit, where I was loaded up with psychotropic medications and mood stabilizers and returned at long last to my own cell. I felt groggy and over-medicated when I got there, but at least I was "home," back in my own place and among my own things. My tablet and my flex pen were still in my cell where I had left them, and everything else seemed in order, too. I wrote a little bit, setting down as much of my recent experience as I could remember. Then I felt my eyes growing heavy and darkness setting in, even though the light in my cell was on, as bright as nebulae in the sleep I settled in.

I woke up to someone shaking me, a flash of something neon pink, the smell of smoke, and for a moment I thought the state had changed its plans and placed me in "Old Smokey," as they call the electric chair in Pennsylvania, instead of strapping me to a gurney and inserting the two IVs into my veins that are used to carry out execution by lethal injection. But I wasn't being executed and it wasn't a prison official who was leaning over me.

It was mum.

Get up, get up, Evelyn screamed.

For a moment, judging from the alacrity in mum's voice and the smoke smell permeating my cell, I thought the prison was on fire. I wondered what I should save, what I could save, if I could even save myself. I thought about this manuscript, of course. But when I looked around to survey my possessions, to see what was up, the gray walls of my cell had receded into yesterday, and I found myself back in a familiar place, staring at the white walls of my room.

I noticed through my heavy-lidded eyes that mum was smoking a cigarette. The ash was the size of two or three erasers. Mum's face was unlined with makeup or mascara and she was wearing a pink bathrobe, one of those Hello Kitty Baby kind that have little kitty faces over the pockets. Her pink slippers had kitty faces, too. I could tell from the waning gibbous moon in the sky outside my window that it was early, very early; the day had dawned iridescent on the horizon but the sun had not yet climbed into the darkly purple sky. The moon was pale and ghostly and the man inside it was missing an ear and part of a jaw. The clock in my bedroom said it was a few minutes before 7.

Get your ass out of bed, mum said.

What's going on? I asked her, blinking disbelievingly at the walls, the moon outside the window, the sky. Mum's neon apparition blurred with the dawning sky, which was becoming pinker and less purple by the second.

That's what's going on, Evelyn said, pointing toward

the doorway.

I was expecting to see a cadre of COs, one of them holding up an IV drip while another pushed a gurney into my cell. Instead, I saw the view from my bedroom, the open doorway, the carpeted hallway leading into the living room at the front of our house in Arlington.

I rubbed sleep from my eyes. Mum leaned over me and shook me again, her harsh pink bathrobe looming like a first-degree burn. One of the kitties on her pockets winked at me, I swear.

Get your ass out of bed, Evelyn said. Now!

I didn't know what was up. My thoughts flashed back to high school and the confrontation I had with her after I dropped out. I remembered her pulling my bedcovers off while I slept, the naked feeling of being exposed. I felt my arms and legs contracting into a fetal ball. Déjà vu all over again, I said to myself.

Look, look, get your ass out of bed and go look, mum said, her finger pointing at some spot beyond the doorway to my room.

I rolled out of bed, and pulled my jeans up over my underwear, and padded out in bare feet to the hall, following Evelyn's pointing figure to a spot on the carpet in the living room when one of my pups had done his business.

Clean it up, she croaked.

I'll take care of it, I said.

Clean it up right now! You know, Evelyn told me, as I went off in search of some paper towels, a rag and some ammonia, you promised me when you brought those dogs into my house that you'd take care of them. You'd feed them and you'd walk them and take them outside to do their business. Now here they are pissin' and shittin' all over my house.

It's one accident, mum, I told her.

You're the accident, she said. The biggest fucking mistake of my life.

I wondered if that was true. It struck me that Evelyn had probably made lots of mistakes in her life. My dad, Sammler, was probably a mistake. Ray was definitely a mistake. In fact, Evelyn had made a thousand mistakes in the men department, and her mistakes didn't stop there. She was the grasshopper in the Aesop's fable about the grasshopper and the ant, idly singing away the summer while the industrious ant was busy gathering and storing winter food. Evelyn was the party girl who didn't understand that the party had moved on without her and no one had given her its new address. In the last analysis, I didn't think I was any more of a drag on her life than she was. It wasn't my fault she lived in a shithole. It wasn't my fault that she was drinking herself to death, that she was miserable and unhappy, that she was growing older by the minute, that any beauty she had ever had in her (well not in her, there was nothing inside, Evelyn was all surface) had begun to fade. I pictured a rose, a Parisian pink one, after all of the petals had dropped off and the only thing left was thorns.

Clean up after your animals, she growled, and pick the shit up off the floor. Then you pick up your shit and get the fuck out of here.

In that déjà vu moment I remembered a promise I had once made to myself.

You better not call the police, I said. You'll be sorry if you do.

You think so? Evelyn said.

Yeah, I do.

Well, we'll see who's gonna be sorry. Evelyn picked up my cell phone from where I had left it in the living room. She started to make a call.

I turned my back to her and walked into my room and keyed in a couple of numbers on the push-button combination on my gun safe. I took out my body armor and put it on and looked around for something to wear over it. I finally settled on my Heroes of Hockey jersey, the one with the stick-holding penguin on its face and the big number 66 on the back.

While I was dressing, I heard Evelyn's voice from the other room.

Uh, yes, This is uh, Evelyn Popovich … I need police to escort my son out. He's a 24-year old. He must have come in drunk last night, and I don't want him here.

I put on my shoes and socks while Evelyn gave the 911operator our address.

I have a 23-year-old boy, 24-year year-old child, she repeated, and I want him out.

I reached into my gun cabinet and took the Mossberg Maverick out and loaded it.

Look, Evelyn said to the 911 operator a third time, I'm just waking up from a sleep and I want him gone.

Are you leavin', she screamed in my direction. Or do police gotta come?

I got my .357 Magnum and loaded it with six 125-grain, semi-jacketed hollow-point bullets. I strapped an ammunition belt over my Heroes of Hockey jersey, right about where the puck meets the penguin's stick. The belt was the combo cartridge type designed to hold

.12 gauge shotgun shells with some extra cartridge loops for the magnum. I put some Speed Loader Swifts on the shotgun shells so I could remove them in pairs and load my Maverick faster. After strapping the belt on, I looked at myself in the mirror. I started back a little when I saw my reflection. My face was puffy from lack of sleep, and I looked haggard and unshaven. My hair was greasy and my eyes lacked their usual shine. If I had seen my mirror image on the street, I might not have been able to recognize it. Are you looking at me? I asked the image staring back at me from the mirror. Are you looking at me?

I removed my AK-47 from the gun cabinet, loaded it, and stood it up in a corner of my room. Then I sat down on my bed and waited.

The clock on my bedroom table said 7:11. Lucky numbers, maybe. I thought of a craps game where someone throws a "seven" or "eleven" and wins. If the time on the clock was my come-out roll, I was in good shape, but I had a sneaky feeling that the "point," the number to be rolled from the pass line, had already been established, making the "seven" and "eleven" on the clock face numbers that couldn't win. Unlucky numbers then.

The doorbell rang. I heard mum answering it. Come and take his ass, she said.

I walked into the living room, the .357 strapped to my hip, the Maverick in my hands.

A police officer was just stepping through the doorway to the house when I walked into the living room.

I don't recall what he looked like. I couldn't tell you if he was handsome or ugly, young or old, tall or short, fat or skinny because, frankly, the only thing I noticed was the uniform and the badge. I knew he was coming for me and that I had lived my last minute in that house. I knew he was gonna take away my guns like Obama and the ZOG wanted.

In the second before his front foot landed on the welcome mat inside the doorway, I swiveled the Maverick up from my hip, pointed it at his head, and fired.

The blast shook the walls of the house, knocking a painting off its hanging hook and sending it crashing to the floor. Plaster loosened by the blast rained down upon my head. The blast was loud enough to do that. The muzzle flash wasn't much, even in the low light, but the blast was damned loud. I had fired the Maverick many times before in the woods outside KG's camp, but I had never fired it inside before, and I had not anticipated just how loud it would sound. My ears rang from the blast. They rang for weeks. Truth of the matter is they're still ringing.

If I had it to do over again, I would have worn ear plugs, not the regular kind, but the special purpose Walker's Game Ear kind that block sounds like a muzzle blast but don't block out the smaller sounds you need to hear, the whispers and the footsteps of the human hunters who may be stalking you. If I had it to do over again, I would have saved some of the money I spent on Coleman lamps and other survival gear and spent it on a Walker Game Ear or a Tactical Ear HD Pro.

Of course, if I had it to do all over again, I wouldn't have shot that cop.

At that moment, in the precise second or two after I shot him, I didn't have time for recrimination or remorse.

I didn't have time because a second uniformed officer was coming through the doorway and this one had unholstered his gun.

I raised the Maverick again and pointed it at the officer's head. In the moment before I fired, I saw his tight-lipped face staring back at me, the furrows on his forehead, the hairs on his head and arms standing on edge. He was about my age, a few years older perhaps, about my height and weight. Although no one would mistake him for me, there was a resemblance. It wasn't quite like looking at a doppelganger self. It was more like looking at one's own reflection in an amusement park mirror but, instead of seeing a grossly distorted image, seeing a reconfigured and reconstructed one, a better self.

I pulled the trigger … and nothing happened.

In the meantime, the officer had pointed his .40 caliber pistol at my chest. He fired. The round pierced my Heroes of Hockey jersey, ripping a hole through the penguin's head. If it had continued through my German Kevlar armor and into my body, it would have struck my heart (assuming, of course, that I have one). A few inches higher, it would have blown my larynx away and severed my spine. A few more inches north, it would have entered my frontal lobe, torn through the midbrain, and killed me. As it was, the bullet flattened against my vest and lodged itself there, failing to penetrate the last layer or two of Kevlar. The shot knocked me backwards, of course, almost carrying me off my feet, and I was left with a raspberry-colored bruise in the spot above my rib cage, a few inches from my nipple, that didn't go away for days.

The shot should have killed me, but it didn't.

After I was sent reeling backward against the wall, I pivoted into the kitchen and tried to clear the Maverick and chamber another round. Breath sounds, mine and his, filled the house. I figured that I had short stroked or short-shucked the shotgun – operator error – and that was why it jammed. While I was attempting to clear it, I heard static from a police radio and the officer yelling something about a cop being down. Code 3! Code 3! he shouted.

The sound of his voice was enough to get me moving again, out of the kitchen, down the hallway, toward my room. As I ran, I laid down some cover fire with my .357.

The officer who was trailing me fired back, his .40 caliber bullets ripping into the drywall. Plaster dust lay suspended like motes in the early morning light. Static crackled on the officer's radio.

I got to my room, and grabbed the AK-47 I had left in a corner. In my pre-siege preparation, I had inserted a loaded magazine into the weapon. All I needed to do now was to move the selector lever off safety, pull back and release the charging handle, aim and fire. I fired bursts of two and three shots through the wall separating me from my pursuer. I could feel blood pulsing in my temples as I fired. The hallway filled with the smell of expanding gases escaping from the gas port on the AK's barrel.

I circled back into the living room, firing bursts from the AK as I went. Unable to match my firepower, the officer was attempting to retreat. The hunter had become the hunted.

When I stepped into the room, he was just a few feet from the open front door. He might have made it too if his fallen partner's body wasn't blocking the exit. If he had shown a little less reverence, by stepping on his partner's back, he may have made it out of the house before I fired. Instead, he reached down and grabbed his partner by the arm and tried to drag him across the threshold. As he reached down, I fired a burst from the AK. Two or three of the rounds struck him in the back, below the collarbone, and under the shoulder. He staggered out of the house.

I stepped over some spent .40 casings and went to a window at the back of the house to make sure no one else was creeping up on me. Then I returned to the front room. Above the din in my ears, which were still reverberating from the Mossberg, the .357 and the AK, I heard the sirens of approaching police cars. I stepped over the officer in the doorway and took a peek outside.

Mum was pacing the driveway in her pink Hello Kitty bathrobe, nervously smoking a cigarette. Her face was as white as the ash on her Kent. She was staring in horror at the second officer, who was lying, face up, on the concrete between the front door and the driveway. He wasn't moving, but I thought he might be playing possum. I went outside, stood over him, and fired a burst from the AK at his head. Pop pop pop pop. Blood spattered sideways at my feet. Who's sorry now? I screamed at mum. She looked at me in gape-jawed disbelief.

I backed away, stepping over the officer lying in the front doorway. It occurred to me that I might need all the firepower I could muster, so I bent down and attempted to remove his gun from his holster. Blood stained the legs of my pants as I kneeled over the fallen officer. I was fumbling with the snap on his holster, which I couldn't quite unfasten, when something flickered on the periphery of my field of vision and I turned, looking across the street at a spot of glitter, the sun's rays bouncing off a windowpane. A cloud passed overhead, momentarily blocking the sun, and I saw a pair of eyes staring out at me from the window of my neighbor's house. A blind flapped shut. I thought about firing a burst from my AK at the window, when a white SUV pulled up to the curb in front of our house.

The operator of the SUV was wearing a police uniform.

I took dead aim and fired three shots at the driver's side of the windshield. Pop pop pop. The recoil from the AK spun me around a bit, and I looked for Evelyn again, but she had disappeared. I refocused my attention on the SUV. The driver had pulled himself out of the driver's seat, and opened the driver's side door of the van. Enough of him was outside the vehicle for me to get a close look at him.

He was black.

None of the things I had done up until this moment had seemed real. Yeah, I knew what I was doing when I killed the first two officers, but the experience was so out-of-body that it didn't seem like I was actually doing it; it was more like watching someone else, someone who looked like me, an automaton self, doing it. I, my out-of-body self, felt gauzy, as if in a trance, as I watched what my automaton self was doing.

This was different.

This time my out-of-body self and I were one, and they took deliberate aim at the black officer, firing off a couple of bursts of 2s and 3s with the AK. Pop. Pop. The shots hit the officer in his central mass. Pop. Pop.

Pop. The bullets slammed into his torso. He had been steadying himself against the car door with his hand, but let go when the bullets struck him, falling, hard, onto the sidewalk.

I was about to squeeze off another round or two when I became aware of someone shooting back. I knew I was being shot at after I felt a jabbing pain in my right thigh and heard a gunshot a split second or so later. (Contrary to what you see on TV and in the movies, you never hear the gunshot until the bullet has passed you or you have been shot because bullets travel faster than the speed of sound. The correct order isn't Bang! Hit! Fall to the Ground! It's Hit! Fall to the Ground! Bang!) Actually, I didn't fall to the ground after I was hit, although I did feel my leg give out on me. The pain was intense – it was as if someone had run a hot poker through my leg.

Of course, at the time, I couldn't focus on the pain. My only thought was to get out of the way. I darted back inside the house, and slid up against a wall. Breathing heavily, I watched the leg of my cargo pants redden with my blood. It occurred to me that I should do something to staunch the flow. I went into the bedroom and took one of my shirts and ripped it into shreds, typing one end of the shirt around my thigh to fashion a make-shift tourniquet. I used the pieces that were left to compress the wound on my leg.

As I was sitting there, on the floor of my living room, I heard sirens blare. It sounded like every frigging cop in the City of Pittsburgh was coming to my house. The proverbial fucking cavalry to the rescue. Not my rescue, of course. I was one of the bad guys. This bad guy felt dizzy and light-headed and was afraid he was going into shock. I was real worried that I might lose consciousness, either from shock or blood loss, and I wished I had paid a little more attention to those survival books I had browsed in the library back when I was on the survivalist kick. Something in my head told me it was important to remain calm, to stay focused and determined to survive. I took the tourniquet off and applied some more pressure to my wound, and after I got the bleeding to stop, I wrapped some gauze I had found in the bathroom around my leg and taped it up real good. When I was done, I took up position at one of the living room windows, and surveyed the perimeter of my house. The black cop was lying on the ground outside his SUV. He was motioning to someone; like a drowning swimmer, he waved his arm in the air three times. An officer I hadn't seen before ran toward him while someone else put down cover fire. I saw a patch of blue sticking out from behind a tree in my neighbor's yard, and fired at it. Pop. Pop. ... Pop Pop Pop. Then I turned my attention back to the black cop on the pavement. The officer who had run toward him was attempting to pull him from the curb where he had fallen. I shot at both of them with the AK. Pop Pop Pop. ... Pop Pop Pop. The officer, the rescuing one, waved his hand at the bullets as if he was trying to swat them away. One of the rounds struck him, and I watched him crumple and go down. When I didn't see him move anymore after he collapsed on the ground, I looked back to my left, pointing the AK at the tree in my neighbor's yard again. While I was watching, something twitched behind it, and I took aim and fired. Pop. Pop. ... Pop. Pop. Pop. Behind the tree outside my window, I saw something drop. I waited for signs of movement, and when I didn't see any, limped over to the sofa. I folded myself down in it, lit a cigarette, and waited for the SWAT team to arrive.

I didn't have long to wait.

I was on the verge of dozing off when I heard a crash on the street outside the house. I ran to the window and saw an armored vehicle pushing the cop cars and the SUV out of the way. Then it lumbered into my yard. I fired three shots from the AK at the windshield of the vehicle, spider webs forming in the glass. The vehicle came to a halt on the front lawn, and I saw a couple of men in body armor and ballistic shields taking up position behind it. A helicopter hovered overhead. Snipers climbed onto nearby roofs. Then all hell broke loose as the SWAT team opened fire.

SWAT bullets tore into the brick and mortar foundation of the house, broke glass in the windows, and pockmarked the walls. I was pointing my AK out of one of the front windows when the barrage began. A sniper took aim at the barrel and literally shot the AK from my hands. The gun skittered across the floor. I thought about trying to retrieve it, but the SWAT gunfire was too withering to enable me to try. Instead of trying to pick up the AK, I retreated, taking cover inside my room and hunkering down behind a dresser.

The gunfire reached a crescendo and abated and I recognized the ring tone from the cell phone in my pocket ("Famous Last Words" by Day of the Sword). Someone was calling me. I figured that SWAT might want to negotiate my surrender so they could come in and cuff me and fly me off in one of the black helicopters circling overhead. I figured that it might be better to die in combat than give up, and I was ready to snarl something to that effect into the phone when the voice on the other end of the line identified itself as a MasterCard representative. Your account with us is seriously delinquent, the speaker said in a voice that sounded more overseas than American. Hey, man, I told the MasterCard representative, you really got me at a bad time. I understand that, sir, the voice said, but your account is seriously overdue and we'd appreciate it if you'd make a payment today. Can you do that, sir? he said. Can you mail a payment? I'd like to, pal, I said, suppressing laughter, but I can't get anywhere near a mailbox right now. You see, I explained, I'm in the middle of a police shootout, and I don't think you should be expecting payment from me any time soon. Matter of fact, I wouldn't count on getting it at all.

That telephone call strengthened my resolve. Let them come and get me, I thought. I thought about Charles Joseph Whitman and how relieved he must have felt when Houston McCoy and Ramiro Martinez reached the observation deck of the UT Austin tower and peppered him with .38 Special rounds and double-ought buckshot. I thought about Seung-Hui Cho, Eric Harris and Dylan Klebold, all of who killed themselves when their rampages were over. I thought about the gunman I had read about before I fell asleep last night, the one who took forty some people hostage and killed a dozen or more of them before turning his .45 on himself. I held my .357 in my hand, staring at it for quite a while, wondering if it would hurt, and then, for no particularly good reason, I ripped the compress off my leg and stuck my index finger in the entrance wound until it started to bleed again.

Like a scribe dipping a quill pen into an inkwell, I put my finger into the wound and used my own blood to write the letter "K" on my bedroom wall. When I was finished with the first letter, I scrawled another "K." Later, after I was taken into custody, a reporter said that I had tried to write "KKK" in blood upon the walls, implying that my two K's were racist symbols, which wasn't true at all. The first "K" I had written was for Keilah, the second for Kathy Cohen, and I was memorializing the two of them, not the Ku Klux Klan. Truth be told, I wasn't thinking about the Klan at all. I was thinking about my own death, and the two women I had loved, or tried to love, and wanted to remember me. I didn't have any sinister agenda. I didn't mean anything more by it than that.

In fact, I called Keilah right after I had written her first initial in blood on the wall. I hadn't spoken to her in years, but her voice sounded exactly the way I had remembered it. Her voice wasn't the sound of money, like that F. Scott Fitzgerald guy described the voice of one of his female characters in a novel, but if it didn't sound like wealth and class, it was still lovely to hear, as sweet as a heart-shaped cherry, and a little sexy, too. It was good to hear Keilah's voice., but it made me go all soft and gushy. I'm dying, I'm dying, I cried into the phone. I told her that I was lying in a pool of blood, that I was sharing my last breaths with her, and that I wanted her to know I loved her, that I had always loved her. I know, I know, she said, giving me a verbal pat on the head. But she didn't say she loved me back. I guess that was to be expected. At least she didn't call me a jagoff for phoning her in the middle of a shootout with the police.

After we hung up, I thought about called Kathy

Cohen, but I didn't have her number, and there was a more important call I had to make. Talking to Keilah while I was holding the .357 in my hands made me recall the time I had thought about killing myself in front of her. I couldn't do it then, of course, and there was no question of doing it now. The police weren't going to bring her to me and they most certainly weren't going to let me go to her. The closest I could get to my preferred manner of death would be to go out in a hail of bullets while Keilah watched it on TV. Of course, I had no idea whether or not she was watching, just as I didn't know what the TV news would cover. Hell, they chose to ignore most of what was going on in the country, in our world today, so why should my demise be any different?

That's when I decided I didn't want to die after all, that I wanted to live to tell my story, this story, the one you're reading now. That's when I looked at the K's on the wall, and said let's write about it, not in blood this time, but in ink as dark as my soul. So I picked up the phone and dialed 911 and asked the emergency services operator if I could surrender. She patched me in to a supervisor and he patched me in to someone else and eventually I got connected to a negotiator and after forty minutes or so of crying and wheedling and other back and forth, I gave myself up.

You shoulda killed him, Evelyn croaked as I was led out of the house in cuffs.

***

The rest of it you know. I was charged with three counts of murder (not the five I thought I had committed) and two counts of attempted murder (for the cops I shot at and only wounded) and a whole shitload of other charges. I didn't plead insanity because Ronnie Silverstein wanted to save all the psychological crap for the sentencing phase of the trial (When I asked her about an insanity defense, she mumbled something about bases for appeal, whatever that meant.)   So I pleaded not guilty, and Ronnie did her honest-to-gosh-darn level best with my defense. I thought she scored big when she got one of the prosecution forensic experts to admit that he couldn't type the DNA of some of the blood stains found around the house (such as that big patch of stain near the recliner), conceding that they didn't belong to any of the fallen officers or to me and suggesting, perhaps, that some unidentified and unindicted gunman quite possibly could have done some of the shooting and the killing. Ronnie also successfully impeached another one of the prosecution witnesses who was testifying about all the bullet holes in the house but didn't know that Evelyn had put some of them there when she scattered buckshot all around the place in her failed suicide attempt. Ronnie even suggested that mum may have played a larger role in the carnage than she was willing to let on or admit, certainly precipitating what had happened, just like she had done with Ray. Ask me, mum played a role in one, two, three, four or more murders, but the prosecution didn't charge her and the jury didn't care. They took long enough to read the jury verdict slip and gobble down their free county lunch before they found me guilty on all counts. They were even quicker to sentence me to death three times, the sentences, as you might imagine, to run concurrently, because you cannot kill a man more than once.

So I was tried, and convicted, and brought here. That's

the ballgame. Now you folks'll have to wait around for another twenty years or more until the state finally kills me. You can curse the powers that be for wasting your tax dollars on that Old Smokey that never gets used and that new lethal injection apparatus that's just sitting there lying in wait. You can vent as much steam as you want, too, about the government-minted money that's being spent on this supermax facility in the middle of nowhere and the legacy costs for pensions and health care for all those correctional officers watching over guys like me. Or maybe you want to take the longer view and write it off as a cost of imperialism, the price you pay for training these guys for future gigs in places like Guantanamo Bay and Abu Ghraib. Whatever, that's up to you. But in the meantime, I'll be eatin' food you paid for and watchin' TV on your dime. That's the plan, anyway. That's what the law has writ.

I have some other ideas. First, you'll be relieved to know I don't have another book in me. This little bastard book can go out on its own, and it isn't going to have any siblings, kind of like myself. Second, I've been thinking a lot lately about Billy Till, and I think I figured out how he done it. All along, I thought he had hung himself by looping a belt strap or a bed sheet up on the ceiling someplace, but I couldn't figure out how. There aren't any air vents up there, and you can't do it from the overhead light. There just isn't anything with holes big enough to thread a bed sheet through. No, I'm certain, Billy hanged himself from some place lower down, perhaps while he was on his knees or even lying on the ground, from the bed rail maybe or that pipe under the sink. I tried it myself a couple of times, in fact, by ripping up a tee shirt and wrapping it around the pipe and my neck, but every time the noose tightened and I felt like I was about to pass out, I'd either pull the noose off my neck or just lift my head up to relieve the pressure. That was the part that's had me stumped. How did he keep himself from involuntarily resisting his own death, how did he suppress that gosh awful will to live all of us have inside ourselves? I was looking around my cell at all the fixture points, staring so hard and so long that I started to get those amoeba-like lines and shapes in my field of vision that one gets when the eyes are tired. I had taken off my glasses and was rubbing my eyelids, when I suddenly realized that I had the answer right there in my hands. Those goddamn clunky glasses I've been wearing since I was a kid were my flight ticket to another America, one up there in the spacious skies, above the purple mountains majesties and across Rush Limbaugh's fruited plain, my portal to the hereafter, so to speak. The good thing about them is that they weren't made of shatterproof polycarbonate like most regular eyeglasses are, and, consequently I was able to break them into pieces by hammering them against the sink. One of the broken pieces had a jagged edge, not sharp enough to open up a vein quite as good as I'd like, but good enough to do the job I had in mind.

I swallowed some of my psychotropic medicine, enough to get me real relaxed, and took my jagged piece of glass, my notebook and my pen and lay down on the floor. Then I wrapped my tee around the pipe and my neck, pulling it good and tight, and jabbed the glass into my wrist. Blood spurted out onto the floor in rivulets. Blood, my blood, stained the open pages of my notebook, dotting my i's and crossing my t's, forming wet asterisks next to the words I've written here.

***

The blood on these pages is yours, too.

***

I figure in the next few minutes or so, I'll have lost enough blood to let me to go slip sliding away into unconsciousness. Then my homemade noose can finish off the job.

So these are my last words.

Sorry all for what I did.

Sorry even more for depriving you of the spectacle of watching me strapped on the gurney and put to death by the state. Closure and all. I understand.

The good news is I'll be gone. Like that cat Yusuf Islam says, you won't be seeing any more leaping and hopping out of me.

The bad news?

This is America, God bless her, and there's a lot more of them like me out there.

Michael Zimecki writes fiction, nonfiction and plays while continuing to work as an attorney. Born in inner-city Detroit, he did turns as a steelworker, advertising copywriter, medical editor and teacher before practicing law.

Michael has written for Harper's Magazine, The National Law Journal, College English, and The Pittsburgh Post-Gazette, among other publications.

His novella, The History of My Final Illness, about the last five days in the life of Joseph Stalin, appeared in Eclectica Magazine. A play, Negative Velocity, about atom-bomb father J. Robert Oppenheimer, is a past winner of the New Playwright's Contest of the Fremont Center Theatre, located in South Pasadena, California.

Michael lives in Pittsburgh, Pennsylvania with his wife, Susan. He enjoys traveling outside the United States, swing jazz, fedoras, and Hardboiled fiction..

Word-of-mouth is essential for any author to succeed.
If you enjoyed Death Sentences, please consider
leaving a review on Amazon.
Even a couple of lines would make a difference
and would be extremely appreciated.

If you enjoyed **Death Sentences** you may want to
check out other exciting books on our website:
http://www.crimewavepress.com
Subscribe to our newsletter and you will be amongst the first
to learn about new **Crime Wave Press** titles and
free advance readers copies.

Crime Wave Press is a Hong Kong based fiction imprint
that endeavors to publish some of the best new
crime novels from around the world.

Founded in 2012 by acclaimed publisher Hans Kemp of
Visionary World and seasoned writer Tom Vater,
Crime Wave Press publishes a range of crime fiction –
from whodunits to Noir and Hardboiled,
from historical mysteries to espionage thrillers,
from literary crime to pulp fiction,
from highly commercial page turners to
marginal texts exploring life's dark underbelly.

Follow us on Facebook:
http://www.facebook.com/CrimeWavePress